BURIED TREASURES
OF THE
ROCKY MOUNTAIN WEST

BURIED TREASURES
OF THE
ROCKY MOUNTAIN WEST

Legends of Lost Mines, Train Robbery
Gold, Caves of Forgotten Riches,
and Indians' Buried Silver

W. C. JAMESON

August House Publishers, Inc.
LITTLE ROCK

Published by August House, Inc.,
P.O. Box 3223, Little Rock, Arkansas, 72203,
501-372-5450.

Printed in the United States of America

10 9 8 7 6 5 4 3 2 1

LIBRARY OF CONGRESS CATALOGING-IN-PUBLICATION DATA

Jameson, W. C., 1942–
Buried treasures of the Rocky Mountain West: legends of lost mines, train rob-
bery gold, caves of forgotten riches, and Indians' buried silver /
W. C. Jameson — 1st ed.
p.   cm.
Includes bibliographical references.

ISBN-13: 978-0-87483-272-3
ISBN-10: 0-87483-272-1

1.Legends—Rocky Mountains Region. 2. Treasure-trove—Rocky
Mountains Region. I. Title.
GR109.J36 1993   93-20602
398.26'0978—dc20   CIP

First Edition, 1993

Executive: Liz Parkhurst
Project editor: Kathleen Harper
Design director: Ted Parkhurst
Cover design: Wendell E. Hall
Typography: Lettergraphics, Little Rock

This book is printed on archival-quality paper which meets the
guidelines for performance and durability of the Committee on
Production Guidelines for Book Longevity of the
Council on Library Resources.

AUGUST HOUSE, INC.   PUBLISHERS   LITTLE ROCK

For LaTonya

Contents

New Mexico

Utah

Wyoming

Selected References *190*

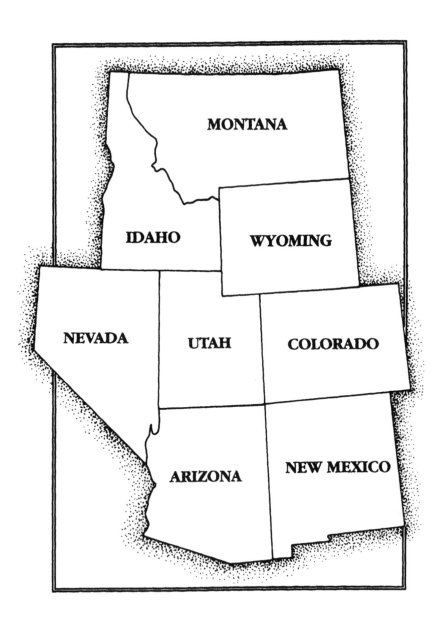

Introduction

The Rocky Mountain West!

The perceptions and images called up by this impressive, environmentally exciting, and culturally diverse geographic region of the United States are many and varied, and the frontier flavor it evokes is unlikely to be matched anywhere else in the United States.

It has provided us with an incredible number and array of myths, legends, folktales, and images relative to the Indian, the mountain man, the cowboy, the gambler, the prospector, and to lost mines and buried treasures. Indeed, the Rockies have been an important geographic source of a number of such tales, both native American and Anglo, which have added considerably to the romantic folklore of this vital place.

ORIGINS

The Rocky Mountains, often referred to as the "backbone of the Americas," is part of a continuous range of diverse origins extending some ten thousand miles from Alaska to the tip of South America. In the United States, this region includes the states of Arizona, Colorado, Idaho, Montana, Nevada, New Mexico, Utah, and Wyoming.

These relatively young mountains of highly varied topography and environment have been subjected to a number of episodes during their formation—some subtle, some extremely violent. The mountains, which effectively divide the United States into two prominent drainage systems, have been folded, cracked, torn apart, shaken, shifted, and uplifted. Volcanic activity has created tall conical peaks as well as vast fields of basaltic rock, a hardened lava that can be found covering extensive portions of the west. Yet other explosive episodes have spewed into the atmosphere millions of tons of ash, which was subsequently deposited in thick layers over many square miles. These mountain-building and environment-modifying activities, all of which are still going on today, are actively accompanied by several natural eroding and sculpting processes that are responsible for the distinctive shapes and settings so often associated with this grand range. These processes include the erosive power of glaciers; the abrasive action of fast-flowing streams; the subtle yet effective gravitational transfer of weathered particles dislodged as a result of frost action, corrosion, and oxydation; the power of the wind, which removes and deposits fine dusts and sand particles. All of these, independently and together, continue the relentless erosion and degradation activities which have been going on for millions of years. This incredible array of land-forming and landscape-shaping mechanisms has created a rather varied and somewhat rugged terrain. Numerous snow- and glacier-capped peaks rise above fourteen thousand feet, with great relief manifested between the mountaintops and the valley bottoms.

Rocks of all classes are found here, products of the various processes of lithogenesis including volcanism, sedimentation, and the extreme heat and pressure of metamorphism. During the formation of these rocks, a separate series of silent processes took place deep below the crust, processes which eventually gave rise to deposits, large and small, of gold and silver. As the older rocks eroded, broke down, and were carried away via erosion, the gold and silver was often exposed, sometimes hinting at vast quantities that remained deep below the surface.

Eventually arriving to cloak this eons-old rock framework were extensive forests. With the coming and going of a succession of varying climatic regimes, these forests progressed through numerous evolutions, eventually culminating in the climax communities found in the region today, which boast a wide variety of species including pines, oaks, and aspens. Within these forest enviroments can be found an equally impressive variety of wild animals, water resources, and scenery.

A more recent agent of change to the Rocky Mountain environments has been man. With his settlements, transportation routes, ranches, and farms, he has imposed a certain cultural character onto the natural landscapes found here. Mining activity, wherein gold, silver, copper, molybdenum, lead, tungsten, zinc, antimony, and other minerals are and were extracted from the solid rock of the range is another imprint of human activity, an imprint that can still be found throughout the Rocky Mountain West from Canada to Mexico.

NEWCOMERS

The mineral wealth so ubiquitous in the Rocky Mountain West was well known to the early native Americans. Here and there, as they found gold and silver, they extracted small amounts for use in fashioning ornaments and jewelry. During the latter part of the sixteenth century, however, the presence of valuable minerals in the Rocky Mountains generated several traumatic events for the Indians: the Spanish, under the leadership of Coronado and others, explored, prospected, and mined gold and silver from dozens of sites in the Rockies. In many cases, local Indians were enslaved and forced to work in the mines. Many died and hundreds of others were driven from their homelands during this insatiable Spanish quest for wealth.

As a result of growing political troubles in Europe and the increasing pressure of Indian uprisings in North

America, the Spaniards were eventually forced to abandon many of their rich mines. The Indians, however, were left with an enhanced awareness of the importance of these shiny minerals to the Europeans.

Beginning in 1804, Meriwether Lewis and William Clark undertook the exploration of a large part of the Rocky Mountain West. Under orders from President Thomas Jefferson, this party, consisting of twenty-six soldiers, two interpreters, and a servant, left St. Louis and followed the Missouri River. After crossing the continental divide, they then explored the Snake River drainage, eventually arriving at the Pacific Ocean.

The explorations and discoveries of Lewis and Clark became well known to hundreds of residents of the East and the slowly growing Midwest. The tales of their travels and the news of abundant land and resources appealed to many, and a fever to migrate into and settle on the lands of the West grew until it could no longer be contained. The abundance of wildlife and the associated opportunities relative to the fur trade soon lured dozens of adventurous men into the far mountains to trap beaver and other fur-bearing mammals. Hats made from beaver fur were in demand in the east and in England, and these new mountain men were hard pressed to meet the initial demand for the exquisite pelts. It was, in fact, these early trappers who originally applied the term "Rocky Mountains" to this vast range.

With the passage of a few years, many of the streams that had yielded thousands of beaver pelts were trapped out. Sometime later, even the demand for beaver hats slacked off, and the glory days of the trappers and mountain men faded into history. Though they no longer plied their trade in the Rockies, these hardy souls left a huge legacy.

In addition to entering the records of history as explorers, Indian fighters, and tellers of tall tales, the mountain men were responsilble for blazing trails that were later to become important routes for westward travelers seeking Utah, Oregon, California, and New Mexico. These intrepid individuals also returned to population centers in the Midwest and the East with stories of the exciting potential of the Rocky Mountains. The aura and subsequent lure of this extensive and largely uncharted wilderness served as a catalyst for more migration. People yearning to explore, to move west, to claim land for their own, to seek new opportunities, and to prospect for gold and silver were captivated and encouraged by the stories, and a steady stream of migrants began to move westward, following the trails into and through the mountains. At first this stream of settlers was but a trickle, but when gold was discovered at Sutter's Mill, California, in 1848, it grew to a river of thousands bent on finding their fortunes, all traveling into and through the Rocky Mountains on their way to the promised land.

Unfortunately, dreams of wealth in the California gold fields came true for but a few, and many of those who were disappointed with their luck in the Golden State returned to the Rocky Mountains through which they had passed earlier. Here many found the gold and silver for which they searched in the rocks of the range and remained to mine the ore, some with great success. As a result, dozens of mining towns sprang up in the mountains, some boasting large populations, concert halls, schools, and libraries. Some of these settlements still exist, but most are now ghost towns of rotted planks, crumbling bricks, and dusty streets, testimony to the relentless pursuit, and ultimately exhaustion, of the mineral resources.

LOST MINES AND BURIED TREASURES

While some commercial mining continues in the Rocky Mountains today, the region has become quite a bit more economically diversified. Farming, ranching, forestry and lumbering interests are common throughout the region.

A major and growing industry is tourism. The abundance of national and state parks and monuments attracts millions of travelers each year to managed campgrounds or hotel and motel accomodations ranging from the plush to the simple. Many go back home, never again to seek the serenity and solitude of the mountains. Some, however, choose to return, remain, or retire there, adding to the ever-growing population in the region.

But even with encroaching civilization, the Rocky Mountains still contain many remote areas, places one can discover and experience only on foot or by horseback, places trod centuries earlier by Indians, Spaniards, explorers, prospectors, and miners—places long since nearly forgotten. In these special locations linger a certain wildness and a mystery often associated with the remote and the unknown. From these places have come many fascinating and mysterious tales of lost mines and buried treasures, tales that had their origins with those same Indians, Spaniards, early propectors and miners, the occasional wandering or lost cowboy, and the outlaw on the run.

To many these stories are just that and nothing more. To others, the stories are relics, legacies if you will, of the long ago occupants of the land—the dreamers, the workers, the discoverers, the survivors, the defeated.

That gold and silver exist in the Rocky Mountains in great quantities is an unarguable fact—it has been proven time and time again. Millions of dollars' worth of ore has been discovered and removed from the range, but millions more likely remains. Some of it has been found and lost. Some has been mined and cached and forgotten. Some has been hidden, the hiders fully intending to return but somehow unable. Much of the wealth in the form of gold and silver ore and bullion is still there, fortunes waiting to be found by the patient and persistent hunter of treasure.

ARIZONA

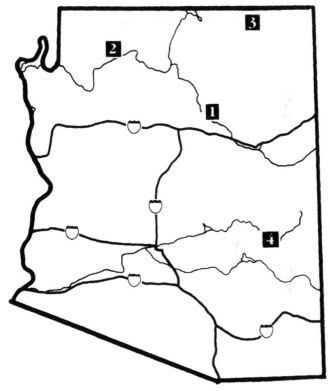

1. Lost Canyon of Gold
2. The Gold Behind the Waterfall
3. Monument Valley Silver
4. The Apache's Mysterious Mountain of Silver

Lost Canyon of Gold

During the latter part of the sixteenth century, large portions of the country west of the Mississippi River were being systematically explored by mounted and well-armed parties of Spaniards. One of the objectives of these forays into the wild and unsettled lands was to locate deposits of gold and silver. Once ore was discovered, mining operations were commenced, small smelters were constructed, and several times a year the accumulated ingots were transported to government headquarters in Mexico City and then shipped to Spain.

Antonio de Espejo was in command of one such party of Spaniards. In 1583, the group entered a maze of canyons located in the southern part of present-day Coconino County near the town of Sedona. Fearing they were lost, de Espejo ordered his men to set up camp while several scouts were sent out to locate a trail that would take them to the open country they believed existed several miles to the north. While preparations were being made for dinner that evening, two members of the party discovered a thick vein of gold along one canyon wall and notified their leader.

Impressed with the quality of the ore, de Espejo decided they should remain in the canyon and mine the gold. During the next few weeks, soldiers were set to work constructing living quarters out of rock and timber, both plentiful in the verdant canyon. In the meantime, a large party of soldiers rode south to procure Indian slaves to work the mine.

Within days, the soldiers returned with a hundred Indians who were immediately put to work excavating the gold from several locations in the canyon. For nearly three months the ore was mined, smelted, and stacked inside one of the shafts, awaiting transportation to Mexico City.

Just as de Espejo was growing comfortable with his mining operation, the canyon was invaded by hostile Indians who resented the enslavement of their brethren. Each day Spanish hunting parties were attacked, and several nighttime raids on the camp killed a dozen soldiers. After losing a number of men and growing more frustrated each day with the increasing guerilla warfare of the Indians, de Espejo decided to abandon the canyon. He and his men loaded up what gold they had accumulated, made several maps of the area, and fled the canyon, returning to Mexico.

With the passage of time, de Espejo's maps showing the location of the rich canyon along with his diary describing the mines were placed in the archives of the Catholic church in Mexico City. Church leaders who came across these documents twenty years later were thrilled with the prospect of riches to be found in the north, so in 1603 they arranged for another party of Spaniards to travel to the canyon and reopen the mines. This was done, and according to church records, a tremendous amount of gold was mined during the next several years.

At the beginning of the seventeenth century, growing difficulties in the Spanish government and the Church began to interfere with various mining activities taking place throughout the American West. The war in Europe demanded manpower and the attention of the Spanish leaders. Dissention within the ranks of the Catholic church also proved distracting. In addition, a general uprising of Indians and the accompanying hostility toward Europeans throughout much of the North American West forced the abandonment of most of the mines operated by the

Spaniards. Eventually all was quiet in the sheltered canyon as, once again, the miners, soldiers, and priests withdrew and returned to Mexico.

In 1719, another group of priests discovered de Espejo's diary and maps in the church archives, and organized another major expedition to the canyon. Accompanying the priests were several mining engineers and a squad of soldiers. As the party passed through northern Mexico, the soldiers captured and enslaved two hundred Opata Indians, chained them together, and marched them 250 miles on foot to the mines, where they were put to work excavating the ore. The priests repaired and moved into the living quarters which remained from the previous expeditions. The Indians, who often worked sixteen hours each day in the mines, slept in the open and were provided poor rations. Many died from exposure, hunger, and overwork.

This highly successful gold-mining operation continued until approximately 1760. During the course of the forty years it was managed by the Spaniards, hundreds of burro loads of gold ingots were transported from the canyon to the church headquarters in Mexico City, enriching the Catholic treasury beyond the wildest dreams of its administrators. Suddenly, however, the canyon was abandoned and no explanation was ever provided by the church; the Spaniards simply left and never returned. Many researchers believe another Indian uprising forced the Europeans to flee southward, but that is only speculation.

The mysterious canyon of gold remained unoccupied, perhaps even forgotten, for almost one hundred years. In 1853, a lone horseman, fleeing a group of Hulapai Indians who killed his three companions while they were prospecting several miles to the south, chanced upon the canyon. As he rode into the defile, the horseman, Clifford Haines, was stunned to discover several rock and log structures as well as evidence of mining activity. After an initial inspection of the area, Haines realized the site had been abandoned for many years but had once apparently accommodated a population of dozens of people. From where he stood among the crude dwellings, Haines could see the openings to several mines in the nearby cliff walls. Inspecting three of the shafts, he retrieved several chunks of rich gold ore and found numerous seams of gold that looked promising. Determined to put together a party of men to return and mine the ore, Haines placed the pieces of gold in his saddlebags and, wary of pursuing Indians, left the area. Eventually reaching Tucson, Haines organized a group of men to accompany him back to the canyon. He made plans to leave within a few days after procuring some supplies, but unfortunately he was killed the next morning when a horse fell on him.

In 1874, a man named John T. Squires arrived in Santa Fe, New Mexico, with a very old and tattered map which purportedly showed the location of several rich gold mines in a remote canyon in Coconino County, Arizona. With a small party, Squires traveled to Arizona and reportedly located de Espejo's lost canyon. They cleaned out and moved into the old dwellings, reopened two of the most promising mines, replaced the rotting timber supports, and rebuilt the crude smelter.

After extracting and smelting a quantity of gold, Squires and company returned to Santa Fe for the purpose of purchasing supplies and mining equipment and hiring several more men to work in the mines. Upon returning to the canyon several weeks later, however, Squires discovered it was now inhabited by nearly a hundred Indians.

The miners had been in the canyon for only two days when the Indians attacked. Squires and two others were several miles away hunting deer when the assault came. All of the miners were killed within minutes and the dwellings were set afire.

As Squires led the hunting party back to the canyon, he saw smoke rising above the clifftops. Suspecting the worst, he ordered his companions to wait while he rode ahead. As he entered the canyon he took in the death and destruction that had just occurred. Quickly scanning the area, he noted the Indians were already sealing the entrances to the mines with rocks and debris. Within seconds Squires was spotted and chased by a half dozen Indians. Spurring his mount, he returned to his fellow hunters and together the three fled from the area.

Squires returned to New Mexico determined to organize a larger, well-armed party, one better prepared to deal with the hostile Indians and reopen the mines. While making plans for a return trip, however, Squires was killed in a gunfight in Taos. The only item found on his body was a map showing the location of the canyon, but it was accidentally burned a few days later.

Around 1889, following the removal of the last of the Indians to Indian Territory or reservations, several members of Squires's original mining party attempted to return to the canyon but were unable to relocate it.

In 1896, a man named William Howard accidentally found the lost canyon of gold. Hired to provide meat for the workers laying track for the Santa Fe Railroad, Howard rode into the canyon searching for game. He entered several of the old, fallen-down dwellings and found numerous articles that had once belonged to members of the Squires party. When Howard related his experiences several months later to two veteran prospectors, they told him of the gold discoveries of de Espejo and Squires. Believing he had surely found the lost canyon of gold, Howard, along with several friends, decided to try to relocate it and reopen the mines. On returning to the region, however, Howard became confused, was unable to recognize pertinent landmarks, and failed to find the canyon.

Howard refused to give up and continued to search for the canyon over the next several years. One day he rode into Flagstaff and announced that he had finally located it. He described the narrow canyon, the old stone and timber structures, and the covered-up mine shafts. Howard confided to several acquaintances that he was in the process of removing some of the rock debris from one of the mine openings and expected to have it cleared within a few weeks. He continued to return to the canyon for several days at a time for nearly a year but stopped providing information to friends. Howard passed away in 1916, and if he ever removed any gold from the old Spanish mine he never told anyone.

In the 1920s, a cowhand entered the canyon searching for strays. Several days later back at ranch headquarters, he reported finding several very old rock and timber structures and claimed to have seen several mine shafts. The significance of the canyon was unknown to him, however, and he never returned.

During the mid-1930s a pilot, flying low over the region, detected several old dwellings at the bottom of a remote canyon in south Coconino County and informed several friends who made a hobby of searching for archeological artifacts. After receiving directions to the canyon from the pilot, they found it and explored the area for a full afternoon. Hoping it would turn out to be ancient cliff dwellings of some kind, the group was disappointed at finding only a few old tumbled-down rock structures.

In 1937, a resident of Virginia who was staying at a guest ranch in nearby Oak Creek Canyon decided to take a long hike through the maze of canyons he knew existed in the region. Carrying a small pack filled with provisions and a camera, he struck out on the trail for an extended journey into the picturesque backcountry. After two days, he wandered into the lost canyon and took several photographs of the old primitive dwellings he found there. Upon his return to the guest ranch, he had his pictures developed and showed them to employees and fellow visitors. An old cowboy who was in charge of the riding stock at the guest ranch saw the photographs and noted the old rock and log buildings. Being familiar with the story of de Espejo's lost mine, he realized the importance of the hiker's discovery. Together, the cowboy and the Virginian attempted unsuccessfully to relocate the canyon.

In 1946, the son of the Virginia photographer, accompanied by a friend, tried to find the lost canyon of gold. Using the father's photographs as a guide to the area, the two men attempted to retrace the route to the canyon. While they were able to identify many of the landmarks in the photographs, they claimed that over the years the character of the region had changed somewhat as a result of forest fires and flash floods. After several days of searching, they too finally gave up.

The search for Antonio de Espejo's rich gold mines located in some remote canyon in south Coconino County continues today. With the passage of time, new forest growth, and the ongoing processes of erosion and weathering, it has become more and more difficult to find the lost canyon. However, it has been rediscovered in the past, and eventually some fortunate treasure hunter will likely stumble onto it and relocate the old mines and the the incredible fortune in gold ore still lying within the rock matrix of the deep canyon walls.

The Gold Behind the Waterfall

Old Tom Watson was a prospector and outdoorsman who spent virtually all of his life in the mountains and canyons of northern Arizona searching for a rich deposit of gold. He always believed he would someday find his fortune and retire to a life of luxury, but in the meantime he was content to wander and explore the remote backcountry.

One day, Tom Watson stumbled upon a phenomenal cache of gold nuggets. In a brief instant his dreams had come true, but he was not destined to retrieve his new-found wealth. Instead, circumstances forced him to abandon the gold and he spent what was left of his life trying to relocate it.

Watson was a tall, thin man of about sixty-five years of age. He was constantly in need of a bath and haircut, but the residents of Flagstaff were always glad to see him when he returned from several months of prospecting in the rugged canyonlands to the north and northwest. Watson would remain in town for a week or two, accepting drinks from friends and sleeping in the livery stable. When he tired of life in the settlement he would eventually purchase a few meager supplies, repack his burro, and head back into the remote parts of the Grand Canyon searching for gold.

During one of his visits to Flagstaff, Watson found an abandoned cabin not far from town. As it was late November and the weather was turning cold, he decided to move into the old weathered structure and remain until spring. The cabin contained nothing in the way of furniture or creature comforts, only boxes of old newspapers, catalogues, and letters. Watson used these papers to start a fire in the hearth each morning.

One cold January morning, Watson grabbed a handful of old letters he intended to use to get a blaze going when he noticed one of them had not been opened. Curious, he opened it. It was to change his life forever.

Watson pulled out a letter dated six years earlier. Accompanying the letter was a crudely drawn map. The missive began "Dear Brother" and related an incredible tale of the discovery and loss of a large amount of gold. The writer had penned the letter from a physician's office in Williams, a small settlement about thirty miles west of Flagstaff. He told of finding a fortune in gold nuggets lying on the floor of a canyon. As he was leaving this canyon with a leather sack filled with nuggets, he was attacked by two men. Fearing the men were after his gold, he threw the sack onto a small ledge behind a waterfall he passed during his flight from his pursuers. Though he shot and wounded one of the bandits, he received two serious wounds himself. Bleeding heavily, he was found by two trappers the next day and carried to the doctor in Williams.

Because of the serious nature of his wounds, the writer expressed the hope that his brother would travel to the canyon, locate the waterfall, and retrieve the gold. Why the brother failed to open the letter will never be known, and Watson instantly realized that, unless the wounded man returned for the gold himself, it must still be there.

As Watson examined the map, he saw that the canyon referred to in the letter was, in fact, the Grand Canyon. Watson knew from personal experience that there were numerous waterfalls in the canyon.

Curious, Watson traveled to Williams to talk to the town physician. He met a Dr. Rounseville who recalled treating a badly wounded man who had been carried out of the canyon about six years earlier. The patient, according to the doctor, was badly wounded and did not survive. Watson realized then that the pack of gold must still lie behind the mysterious waterfall.

Following the directions on the map, Watson traveled to Havasupai Canyon, a deep, secondary erosional scar which is part of the Grand Canyon complex. As he undertook his search, he realized that the map was quite imprecise in the placement of landmarks and locations, and had difficulty interpreting it. Using the map as well as his intuition, Watson explored the canyon for almost a year before returning to Flagstaff for supplies. He found several waterfalls in the canyon, but none quite fit the description of the one mentioned in the letter.

On a subsequent trip into the canyon, it occurred to Watson that some waterfalls only flowed during certain times of the year when the snow was melting. This made the search more difficult and frustrated the old prospector to the point that he almost gave up. Then one day in June, 1914, Watson was leading his burro east along the old Tanner Trail on the floor of the canyon when he heard the sound of water falling in the distance near a point where he had never seen water before. Curious, he investigated and was surprised to find a waterfall located approximately seven hundred feet up the wall of a side canyon. Deciding this would be the last waterfall he would investigate before abandoning his search, Watson left his burro to graze as he climbed the steep rocky slope to the waterfall. Standing close enough to the cascading water to be sprayed by the mist, Watson suddenly realized it fit the description provided by the letter writer. From where he stood, the old prospector could barely discern a small opening behind the sheet of falling water. Poistioning himself somewhat precariously on the slope, he leaped through the waterfall and landed on a narrow rock shelf in a dark, cool recess located immediately behind it.

Using his body as a shield from the spray, Watson lit a match and for a brief instant the small chamber was illuminated. What the old prospector saw made his heart leap, for on the rocky ledge was a dense layer of gold nuggets reflecting the dim light of his sputtering match. As he bent low for a closer look, he noted that the leather sack that once transported the gold had all but rotted away.

Watson estimated that nearly forty pounds of nuggets were spread across the small shelf, a veritable fortune for him if he could remove it and transport it to Flagstaff. As he sat among his newfound wealth, he decided to return to his burro to retrieve his saddlebags, into which he intended to pack the gold. Placing a handful of nuggets into one of his hip pockets, the old man rose on the precarious ledge, ready to leap back through the falls. Just as he stood up in the low-ceilinged chamber, however, Watson's foot slipped on the slick rim of the ledge. He tumbled downward onto the rocky slope below, then slid and rolled all the way to the bottom of the canyon.

Watson lay unconscious, broken, and bleeding on the floor of the canyon for nearly six hours. When he awoke, the sun had long since set and the only light came from the stars. As his burro nibbled on the sparse grass growing in the narrow valley only a few feet away, Watson attempted to struggle to his feet. It was then that he discovered he had broken his left leg just below the knee.

Slowly and painfully, Watson crawled to a pile of driftwood, selected two relatively straight and sturdy sticks and, using his shoelaces, fastened a crude splint to his shattered leg. Though overcome with incredible pain and nausea to the point of nearly passing out, Watson managed to climb onto his burro and ride out of the canyon. About six hours later he arrived at the ranch of Martin Buggelin, where he was taken in and cared for.

Several days later, when the rancher believed Watson was well enough to travel, he transported him to a physican in Flagstaff where it was discovered gangrene had set in. The doctor was able to save the leg, but it was nearly four months before Watson was able to walk without the use of crutches.

Although riding brought him great pain, Watson never lost his enthusiasm for returning to the canyon bottom and retrieving the cache of gold nuggets behind the waterfall. Because of his injured limb, however, he was forced to remain in Flagstaff until more healing took place.

Finally, in November of 1915, Watson had recovered enough to reenter the canyon. In the company of a friend named Roy Scanlon, he rode along the Tanner Trail to the area where he believed the waterfall to be, but it could not be found. It may have been because the season was abnormally dry and no surface water was apparent, or it may have been that Watson was simply lost, but his resultant frustration at not being able to relocate the gold had a disturbing effect on the old prospector who was now nearly seventy years of age.

Watson sincerely believed he was close to the lost waterfall, but was unable to determine in which direction to search. One night in camp while Scanlon was out gathering firewood, the despondent Watson placed the barrel of a carbine in his mouth and, using a short stick to activate the trigger, blew his brains out.

The fortune in gold nuggets undoubtedly still reposes in the small, open chamber behind an out-of-the-way seasonal waterfall someplace in the Grand Canyon near the old Tanner Trail. Because of the vastness of this deep gorge, not many are willing to undertake a search of this magnitude. In truth, there are very few people alive today who are even aware of the long-lost cache. Since Watson's last fatal visit to the canyon in search of the elusive waterfall, no one has ever attempted to find the gold.

Monument Valley Silver

Monument Valley, located in northeastern Arizona near the Utah border, is a picturesque environment dominated by sandstone mesas and buttes, once the homeland of the Navajo and Ute Indians. For years, white settlers heard tales of rich silver ore to be found in the valley, but geologists and prospectors scoffed, claiming that the precious metal could not possibly be associated with the sedimentary rock that makes up so much of this region. In spite of what the experts said, Navajo Indians were known to have mined silver from this area for several generations to make the bracelets, rings, and necklaces for which they were famous. The silver, according to the Indians, was so pure and rich that it wasn't necessary to refine it, that it could be worked as it came directly from the rock.

Longtime Colorado prospector John Merrick heard the stories of silver being located in Monument Valley. Intrigued, he decided to investigate. Teaming up with a young man named Mitchell, Merrick acquired some supplies, pack animals, and equipment and went in search of the precious metal in the fall of 1879.

During this time the Navajo and Ute Indians who inhabited Monument Valley were quite hostile to white intruders. Many who entered the realm of the red man were attacked, killed, and horribly mutilated as an example to others who might dare to cross the region. Carefully avoiding the Indians, Merrick and Mitchell explored Monument Valley in the area of Skeleton Mesa for several weeks before finally locating the silver. The mine was somewhat unimpressive—a low, narrow shaft that extended into some precariously weathered rock for only a short distance. At the end of the shaft, however, Merrick discovered an amazingly rich seam of almost pure ore. Within a few days, the two men dug out enough of the silver to fill several leather packs.

Merrick and Mitchell returned to Durango, Colorado, had their silver formally assayed, and learned it was nearly pure. Enthused by the prospect of great wealth, the two men purchased more supplies and within a few days were on their way back to Monument Valley.

Merrick and Mitchell worked hard in the small silver mine for about three months, following the vein of ore deeper into the rock. In time they accumulated enough silver to fully load three stout mules. As the two men were beginning to believe they would soon retire to a life of wealth and luxury, their luck took a turn for the worse— they were discovered by the Utes.

For several days, the two miners had noticed Indians observing them from afar. Each day the number of watchers increased, and each day they grew bolder, venturing closer to the camp. Worried that an attack was imminent, Merrick decided to take what silver they had accumulated and leave the area at the first opportunity. The next morning following breakfast, the two men loaded the mules with their ore and equipment and rode away from Skeleton Mesa. Behind them came the Utes, slowly closing up the distance.

About an hour later, the two miners rounded a turn in the trail and were surprised to see about twenty Ute horsemen in front of them, blocking their passage. The leader of the Indians, an evil-looking, squat Indian named No-Neck, rode up to Merrick and Mitchell. No-Neck had a reputation for despising whites and swore to kill all that entered his domain. As the chief stopped in front of the two men, the remaining warriors slowly circled the trio.

Using sign language, No-Neck demanded tobacco from the two men. Merrick, believing their safety lay in demonstrating courage rather than giving in to Indian demands, refused and ordered No-Neck and his braves to allow them to proceed. At the signal from the scowling Indian, the mounted warriors fired arrows into Merrick and Mitchell. The two men never had a chance. Mitchell, pierced by more than a dozen arrows, toppled from his horse and was dead before he hit the ground. Merrick, impaled by at least eight arrows, spurred his horse and raced through the line of Indians. He rode for three miles until his mount finally gave out and dropped. Several Utes who trailed Merrick found the seriously wounded man crawling across the stony desert about forty yards from his dead horse. For the next half hour the Indians used the dying miner as target practice for their lances.

No-Neck and his followers took the horses, mules, saddles, equipment, and what few canned goods the two miners were packing. Cutting loose the leather sacks filled with silver, the Indians let them drop to the desert floor next to the body of Mitchell. As the Indians rode away, the desert winds were already shifting the loosely consolidated sands, blowing them along the desert floor to accumulate on the windward side of objects lying in their path. Several months later when a party of soldiers passed through Monument Valley, they discovered the grisly skeletons of Merrick and Mitchell partially buried in the sand, still clothed and booted. Within inches of Mitchell's body were several rotted leather sacks that contained a fortune in pure silver ore.

The story of Merrick and Mitchell and their rich mine was soon spread throughout much of the Southwest, inspiring many to search for it. Those who attempted to enter Monument Valley, however, were driven away by the Indians.

One adventurous soul who was not deterred by the threat of hostile Utes was Cassidy Hite. Hite not only entered Monument Valley, he spent his days in search of the mysterious Indian silver mine from which Merrick and Mitchell dug a fortune in ore. Hite, incredibly, somehow managed to make friends with the local Navajo Indians, who in turn afforded him some protection from the hostile Utes.

One day Hite was searching for the mine in the company of a Navajo companion. While the two were exploring the area around Skeleton Mesa, the Indian picked up a small black rock and showed it to the prospector, who immediately recognized it as silver.

For the next three months, Hite concentrated his searches in the Skeleton Mesa area and one day was rewarded by the discovery of a leather sack filled with pure silver nuggets. Hite presumed Merrick and Mitchell had accidentally dropped the sack while fleeing from the region two years earlier.

Further searching yielded only discouragement, and Hite decided to abandoned his efforts to locate the mine. Weeks later, seated at a campfire with an elderly Navajo, he listened as the old man told the story of journeying to a small silver mine when he was a young warrior. The mine, he told Hite, was located near Skeleton Mesa and he had made trips there to dig out a small amount of silver which he used to fashion ornaments. According to the Indian, the silver was so pure it could be extracted with a knife. When Hite pressed the old man for directions to the mine, the Indian told him the location was a secret known to only a few Navajos. Hite eventually left Monument Valley, never to return.

Several Indians living in or near Monument Valley were interviewed in 1988 about the lost silver mine. Except for one elderly Navajo, none had ever heard the tale. The old man related that the existence of the mine was at one time known to a few older Indians, but its location has long since been forgotten. All the old man knew was that the silver mine was supposedly located near Skeleton Mesa.

The Apache's Mysterious Mountain of Silver

During the 1840s, white settlers in east-central Arizona were surprised to discover that the Apache Indians were using silver instead of lead to manufacture bullets for their rifles. This first came to light when a wagon train, traveling from Missouri to southern California, was attacked near Carrizo Creek. No one was killed, but following the skirmish the train scout dug two silver bullets out of a saddle that had been hit. While many members of the party wanted to remain in the area and attempt to learn the origin of the silver, the hostile nature of the Apaches precluded a lengthy stay.

About twenty years later, a young Mexican named Juan Encinas was captured near Tucson by some far-ranging Apaches and was taken north to an Apache stronghold near the White River. During his ensuing seven years of captivity, Encinas was forced to gather silver for the Indians for use in making bullets. One morning, Encinas escaped while most of the warriors were out on a raid. Barefoot and without food, he walked southward through the desert until, several days later, hungry and exhausted, he was picked up by a small party of Mexican miners near the Sonoran border. While they nursed him back to health, Encinas told the miners of his seven years as a slave. He related how the Indians took him to a place he called

"Silver Mountain," where a large number of silver nuggets were scattered across the ground and could easily be picked up by hand. He also claimed that there was a very thick vein of the ore that extended well over a hundred yards across bedrock and apparently penetrated deep into the mountain. The miners were impressed, and when Encinas recovered several weeks later, they asked him to guide them to Silver Mountain.

After traveling to the north for several days, the party entered Apache country. They were immediately spotted by the Indians and, because the Mexicans were poorly armed and in fear of the warring Apaches, they were easily repulsed and soon returned to Mexico.

In 1890, Pedro Encinas, a nephew of Juan, led a second group of miners back into Apache country. Encinas possessed a map he claimed was drawn by his uncle, that purported to show the exact location of Silver Mountain.

During this time, however, the region in which the mountain was supposedly located was inside the boundaries of the newly established San Carlos Indian Reservation. After introducing himself to W.J. Ellis, the agent in charge of the reservation, Encinas was told that he would be allowed to search for the silver, but he would not be permitted to remove any of the ore from government land.

For several weeks, Encinas and his party camped on the reservation and searched for the mountain. Finally, one day they found it! It was just as Juan Encinas described it—biscuit-sized silver nuggets were lying everywhere and a truly impressive vein of rich ore could be seen snaking along a granite outcrop for dozens of yards. Encinas gathered several samples of the ore, returned to the reservation headquarters, and presented them to the agent. Encinas told Ellis he would abide by his promise not to remove any of the ore from the reservation and would return to Mexico. He also said that if the reservation were to be opened up to mining sometime in the future, he would appreciate being informed. Ellis agreed to contact the Mexican should the policy be changed. As Encinas and his party were preparing to leave, the agent asked the Mexican for directions to Silver Mountain. Encinas refused to part with any information, but informed Ellis that the agent would be considered for a share should permission to remove the ore ever be granted. With that, Encinas returned to Sonora.

Years later, the San Carlos Reservation was temporarily opened up to prospecting, but Ellis was no longer living and Encinas was never informed. In fact, once Encinas returned to Mexico, he was never heard from again.

Others familiar with the story of Silver Mountain have searched throughout the San Carlos Reservation. While a small amount of the ore has been located, the great quantities described by Juan Encinas have eluded everyone.

Around 1940, a resident of Salt River named L.K. Thompson was being interviewed by a newspaper reporter about his experiences as a young man in Arizona. Thompson, it turned out, was a brother-in-law to Pedro Encinas and had accompanied him on the 1890 expedition to the San Carlos Reservation. Thompson was with Encinas when Silver Mountain was discovered, but claimed the Mexican misinformed Indian agent Ellis when he told him it was on his reservation land. The mountain, according to Thompson, is actually located forty miles due east of the San Carlos Reservation and just inside the boundary of the old White Mountain Apache Reservation. Thompson would not explain why Encinas deceived the agent.

When asked why he did not return to Silver Mountain to retrieve some of the ore, the old man said he always believed the mountain to be cursed and was afraid something bad would happen to him or to his family. He said it was not worth the risk.

According to L.K. Thompson, the mountain is in a remote area, seldom, if ever, visited by anyone. The silver nuggets, he said, still cover the ground just as they did when Encinas visited the area decades earlier.

COLORADO

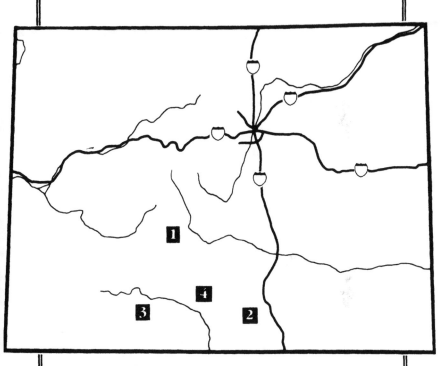

Crazy Woman Gold

In 1901, William C. Fallon accidentally discovered an old newspaper article concerning a long-lost gold mine somewhere on or near Sheep Mountain in Gunnison County. Fallon's discovery revived a fascinating tale of a fortune in gold found and lost, and initiated a search for what must have been an incredibly rich vein of ore.

One summer afternoon while seated in the back yard of his Durango home, Fallon saw a snake fall out of a tree onto the roof of his house. The snake crawled into a hole which led into the attic, and Fallon knew he would have to find the serpent and get rid of it.

As Fallon crawled around the attic in search of the snake, he encountered hundreds of old newspapers left by the previous owner. After thirty minutes of fruitless searching, Fallon paused to rest and happened to notice a story in one of the papers, dated 1860, about a woman who had confessed to killing her husband and leaving his body in the mountains. As he read on, Fallon learned that the dead man had earlier discovered a very rich ledge of gold, a lode which was never seen again after his murder.

The woman named in the article was Dora Tucker. She had arrived in Central City from Independence, Missouri, with her husband George Cyre. Cyre was a printer who found a job with a Central City newspaper. Dora was twenty-two years old, newly married, and fascinated yet terrified by the vast spaces and rugged mountain ranges of the Colorado West.

After a year, Cyre moved a few miles east to Golden and went to work for another newspaper. Within days, the printer got into an argument at a local tavern and was stabbed to death. Dora Cyre, after being married for just slightly more than a year, was now a widow.

Fearful of being alone in a strange land, Dora took another husband within a month. A hard-rock prospector named Clem Tucker courted the widow and won her hand. Two days after the wedding, the bride and groom traveled southwest to Sheep Mountain, where Tucker believed he would find gold and strike it rich.

After the first week in the mountains, Dora realized she had made a terrible mistake. Tucker forced her to tend the primitive camp and help him dig for gold. When she complained of being tired, the prospector beat her mercilessly, often leaving her unconscious. When Dora told her husband she was unhappy and that she wanted to return to Golden, he informed her that if she left him he would find her and kill her.

One morning Tucker noticed that one of his horses had strayed from camp and he set out to find it. As he was searching for the animal in a nearby canyon, he noticed an odd glimmer in a rock outcrop next to the trail. On closer inspection, Tucker discovered an eight-inch-thick vein of quartz laced with almost pure gold.

Tucker spent the next few weeks digging the gold from the outcrop and returning it to the camp, where he showed it to Dora. He told her that his strike was very rich, perhaps worth millions, but that he would have to travel to Denver to obtain supplies and mining equipment in order to excavate it more efficiently. He told her they would leave the mountains in about a month, following the accumulation of enough ore to fill several flour sacks.

Dora could not bear the thought of remaining with the brutal Tucker for another month. That evening as she prepared her camp bedding, she watched the prospector bury the fruits of the day's mining activites. She estimated that several thousand dollars' worth of the gold was cached in the shallow hole he excavated just beyond the glow of the campfire. Presently, Tucker crawled into his own bedroll and fell asleep.

Lying awake, Dora decided to attempt an escape from her miserable circumstances. Although she feared becoming lost in the mountains and was terrified of the Indians who lived in the region, she could not bear another day of beating and humiliation from her husband. Slipping quietly from camp, she unhobbled one of the horses and led it about a hundred yards away before mounting it and riding away in the darkness.

All night long the frightened woman guided the horse along the dark trail. Every sound she heard scared her—the wind rustling in the trees, the calling of birds, the scamper of squirrels and chipmunks. By morning the harried woman was on the verge of a breakdown, but her craving for freedom was so great that she forced herself to push on. When Dora arrived at the sloping foothills that extended eastward toward the plain, she began to relax a bit and hoped to find a rancher or traveler who might be able to help her.

But luck was not with Dora. Just as she was beginning to experience some sense of relief as a result of her successful escape, her horse lost a shoe and immediately went lame. All day long she rode the limping animal, until she found a small spring. Exhausted and thirsty, Dora drank copiously of the fresh water and fell asleep immediately.

Dora dozed fitfully until dawn. She gradually came awake and was ready to resume her journey, when her heart leaped in fright as she gazed at the figure of Tucker standing over her! Before she could get up, the prospector began beating her with his fists until she finally lapsed into unconsciousness.

Dora awoke around sundown. Afraid of another beating, she feigned sleep as she watched her husband prepare camp for the evening. Tucker had followed her out of the mountain, leading a pack horse loaded with several flour sacks filled with gold ore. Through half-closed eyelids, Dora watched as Tucker unloaded the ore from the horse and placed it next to the fire, where a pot of coffee was simmering. After laying out his bedroll, Tucker set his rifle against the bole of a nearby tree, drank a cup of coffee, and went to sleep.

For several hours Dora watched the sleeping figure as a multitude of confusing thoughts raced through her mind. Fearful of another beating at the hands of the cruel prospector in the morning, she moved noiselessly toward the rifle. Seconds later, she placed the muzzle of the weapon against Tucker's sleeping head and blew his brains out.

The report of the rifle startled the horses, which fled into the night. On the verge of going completely insane, Dora Tucker dropped the rifle and began walking away from the camp, unmindful of anything save getting away.

Three days later, Dora was found by a small band of Ute Indians. When she told them she was walking to Golden, the Indians placed her on a spare mount and escorted her to the outskirts of the town. That afternoon Dora Tucker—shaking, disheveled, and babbling incoherently—walked into the small Colorado town she had left several months earlier with her new husband. Realizing her plight, several compassionate church women took the troubled Dora in and cared for her.

For two months, Dora Tucker spoke not a single word to anyone, causing many to believe she was a mute. Presently, however, she began to speak to a kind woman named Sarah Gibson, the wife of the editor of the *Western Mountaineer*. As she came to trust Mrs. Gibson, Dora related the incredible tale of her short marriage to Tucker, the discovery of the rich ledge of gold somewhere on Sheep Mountain, and her harrowing escape to Golden.

Editor Gibson, fascinated by Dora's account, organized an expedition into the mountain in search of the gold. Using directions provided by the woman, who never actually saw the ledge, they explored the area for three weeks before giving up and returning to Golden. They attempted to obtain clearer directions from Dora, but by now the poor woman had gone completely insane and been committed to an institution. The story of a fortune in lost gold related by the crazy woman eventually faded from the minds of most of the area citizens.

In 1896, two men who were riding across the foothills toward Sheep Mountain to do some prospecting stopped to camp at a small spring located about fifteen miles from the mountain. Not far from the spring, they found a skeleton and an old rusted rifle. Examining the skull, they saw that the head had been blown apart by the blast of a large-caliber rifle, most likely the one that lay nearby. Without realizing it at the time, the two prospectors had discovered the remains of Clem Tucker.

The next morning, as the two men were preparing to continue their journey to the mountain, one of them picked up a piece of gold-filled quartz. Other pieces were quickly found, enough to fill a small leather sack. It is surmised that the flour sacks carrying Tucker's gold had long since rotted away, exposing the piles of gold to the elements and allowing them to become scattered across the ground. Had the two men searched the site more diligently they would likely have recovered enough gold to make them both wealthy. Instead, they believed they had found only what the dead man had carried in a pocket.

William C. Fallon, on reading the account of the lost gold mine, decided to seach for it himself. Over the next twenty years, he rode to Sheep Mountain on several occasions looking for the fabulous ledge of gold. Though he was unsuccessful, Fallon kept a journal of his trips and explorations which he gave to his son, George. When Fallon passed away in 1931, George, reading the account of the gold and Dora Tucker, became convinced of the existence of the mine and undertook several expeditions in search of it. For eleven years he combed the environs of

Sheep Mountain, but had no more success than his father. The younger Fallon eventually gave up the search at the onset of World War II.

Once again, the story of the lost ledge of gold and the crazy woman faded from memory and would likely have been completely forgotten except for a recent, important discovery.

A pair of hikers, after returning to Denver from a trip to Sheep Mountain, showed several friends a half dozen pieces of glittering quartz richly laced with shiny metal. They told their friends they dug the curious-looking rock from a thin outcrop in a remote canyon in the mountain. When informed they had discovered gold, the two hikers grew excited and planned a return trip.

For two weeks they searched for the canyon that contained the golden ledge, but never relocated it. More trips are planned, but for now the gold remains elusive.

Recluse Goatherder's Secret Gold Mine

One of the most talked about and sought after lost gold mines in Colorado is associated with mysterious goatherder Alex Cobsky. Cobsky, a quiet recluse, pocketed hundreds of thousands of dollars as a result of mining large quantities of gold from his secret diggings. His mine apparently still contains a great deal of gold, and it is presumed he cached his earnings somewhere deep within the shaft, but its location has been a mystery for more than a century. At one time this gold mine was considered to be the richest in all of Colorado, but the goatherder's passion for secrecy has also made it one of the most challenging to relocate.

The amazing story of Cobsky's gold mine begins in 1869, when one Jack Simpson, a well-known prospector and miner, led two heavily laden burros up to the hitch rail in front of a smelter near Walsenburg in south-central Colorado. Simpson unloaded several packs of gold ore from the animals and astounded the smelter operators with its purity. Before leaving, Simpson sold his gold for around twenty thousand dollars, an incredible fortune at that time.

Several weeks later, Simpson arrived once again at the smelter with another load of gold. This time, several area miners gathered around him and tried to pry from him information about the source of the rich ore, but all they learned was that the prospector's camp was located some-where on Silver Mountain, a few miles northwest of the small town of La Veta. A few men attempted to follow Simpson back to his diggings, but anticipating such action, he took great pains to cover his trail. After his next trip to the smelter, Simpson had accumulated a total of nearly ninety thousand dollars. He was already one of the weal-thiest men in southern Colorado, with the prospect of becoming a millionaire. Simpson was beginning to feel like the luckiest man in the world.

But luck did not remain long with Jack Simpson. On his way back to the secret mine following his third trip to the smelter, he was attacked and killed by Indians. His body was found several weeks later by a group of prospectors.

Learning of Simpson's death, several adventurous in-dividuals entered the wild environs of Silver Mountain in an attempt to locate his rich mine, but none was successful. Interest in the lost mine soon began to wane, and it was all but forgotten until 1901. On a bleak and windy February day of that year, a tall, rangy, and white-bearded man named Alex Cobsky arrived at a Pueblo smelter with three pack horses heavily loaded down with gold. That after-noon, Cobsky, a stranger, rode away with nearly forty thousand dollars in his pocket. Though he never knew it, the story of his incredible gold transaction made newspaper headlines throughout the West.

Cobsky had arrived in the Silver Mountain area four-teen years earlier from Ohio, and grazed goats on the grassy foothills which extended from the mountain. He was quite content with his lot in life, and had no desire for wealth, preferring to live a simple and quiet pastoral life far from throngs of people. But the reclusive goatherder's life changed dramatically when he accidentally found the lost Simspon mine in a remote canyon in the mountain.

For the next several years, Cobsky would ride out of Silver Mountain once every four or five months leading three pack horses loaded down with gold. After exchanging

43

his ore for cash at a smelter either in Walsenburg or Pueblo, he would treat himself to a fine meal in town and begin the return trip just past sundown. It was concluded by many that Cobsky had located the lost Simpson mine and, though many tried to follow him, he was adept at laying false trails and eluding his trackers.

It is estimated that during the years that Cobsky transported his gold to the smelter, he accumulated nearly half a million dollars. Because he was a frugal man and obviously did not trust banks, it was presumed that he hoarded virtually all of this money somewhere near his residence.

Where Cobsky lived on Silver Mountain was a mystery to all except for T.C. Gibbons. Gibbons was fourteen years old when he first met Cobsky at the goatherder's cabin deep in the mountain. The young Gibbons was on a hunting trip with his father and his older brother. When T.C. grew weary from the hike up long canyons and across ridges, he was left behind to wait until the others returned for him.

Cobsky encountered Gibbons sitting on a log near the trail and invited him to his cabin. As soon as the boy entered the log structure, he saw the mine! The back wall of the cabin was the rock face of the canyon wall, and there in the middle of it was the opening to the shaft.

Cobsky, apparently at ease with the young Gibbons, told the boy about his gold mine. Lighting a candle, Cobsky escorted the youngster into the shaft and showed him an iron door fitted expertly into the rock walls about twenty yards from the entrance. With some pride, Cobsky explained to Gibbons that beyond the door was enough gold to support a kingdom, but there were so many cleverly designed traps that anyone who managed to get past this formidable obstacle would be in danger of instant death at almost any location along the tunnel. Although in later years Gibbons never revealed the nature of the traps inside the shaft, rumors abounded that they consisted of

44

dynamite, deadfalls, bear traps, and even poisonous snakes.

After Gibbons returned home with his father and brother, he remained friends with the reclusive Cobsky and visited him often over the years. Yet he kept the location of Cobsky's mountain residence a complete secret.

One day in 1937, after Cobsky had converted several loads of gold into cash at the Walsenburg smelter, he was leading his pack animals back to Silver Mountain when he was struck by a speeding autmobile and seriously injured. With a severely broken leg and numerous internal injuries, Cobsky was transferred to the hospital at Pueblo, where he spent the next year barely clinging to life.

During his stay at the hospital, the old miner was visited by many people who wished to learn the location of his secret gold mine, but he steadfastly refused to provide any information. Gibbons was a frequent visitor and remained loyal to the old man until his death approximately a year following the accident.

After Cobsky's death, several parties intent on locating the secret mine and the old cabin searched the mountain and its canyons, but each and every expedition was a failure. Although Gibbons could have led anyone directly to the mine, he refused every invitation to do so in part out of loyalty to his friend and in part because he feared the dangerous traps that lay beyond the iron door.

With the passing years, Cobsky's log cabin has no doubt fallen to ruin on the canyon floor. Although many have searched, it is doubtful that the shaft containing the rich vein of gold ore, along with Cobsky's approximately half a million dollars in cash, has ever been found. And should the mine eventually be rediscovered, the finders must exercise extreme caution when venturing beyond the iron door for, though much time has passed, many of Alex Cobsky's traps may still function and thus jeopardize the lives of any who seek to retrieve his gold.

Treasure Mountain Millions

Deep in the San Juan Mountains in what is now Archuleta County, an astounding hoard of gold ore, perhaps fifty million dollars' worth, lies buried in a deep, abandoned mine shaft. The gold, fruit of the labor of Spanish miners, was hidden prior to their quick departure from the region as a result of continuous attacks from Indians. This fortune in gold has been the object of innumerable searches for over two hundred years, but most of the original signs and landmarks have long since disappeared. The search continues, and all who have studied this legend are convinced the treasure is still cached deep underground, awaiting discovery by some determined and patient treasure hunter.

Near the end of the fifteenth century, Spanish explorer Juan de Onate established a settlement in the Rocky Mountain wilderness near the present-day Colorado-New Mexico border, not far from the town of Chama. From this settlement, parties of explorers, prospectors, and miners, all accompanied by soldiers, fanned out across the countryside searching for precious metals which they intended to mine and ship to Spain to finance the country's economy and its war efforts in Europe. Many locations rich in gold and silver were discovered and mined, but one of the most prosperous was found in the San Juan Mountains.

Due to a lack of manpower sufficient to carry out the mining operation and defend the region against constant Indian attacks, the Spaniards were forced to abandon the promising San Juan location. Years later, after returning to the European continent, one of the miners who accompanied the expedition filled several journals with tales of the great amounts of gold that had been discovered, and provided landmarks and routes to the location.

Around 1765, a Frenchman discovered the journals of the Spanish miner in a monastery and became enthused at the prospect of locating and excavating the plentiful gold. The Frenchman worked ceaselessly acquiring backers, and over a period of four years was finally able to finance and equip a three-hundred-man party consisting of geologists, miners, laborers, and armed guards. In 1770, the group landed at New Orleans, purchased supplies along with nearly four hundred horses, and undertook the long journey to the San Juan Mountains far to the northwest.

Months later, following the excellent descriptions found in the journal, the Frenchmen arrived at the precise location at which the Spaniards had discovered gold over a century and a half earlier. Excitedly, the men went immediately to work and soon accumulated an impressive store of rich gold ore, both from the abandoned mine shafts and from panning the local streams. In addition, several more veins of gold were discovered, and before long about a half dozen new shafts were being excavated in the mountains over an area that consisted of several square miles. As the ore was taken from the mines, it was separated from the quartz rock and smelted into ingots.

The leader of the French expedition eventually established a headquarters just west of the present-day town of Summitville and located on a mesa-like portion of the southern slope of Treasure Mountain. To this headquarters were delivered the gold ingots, which were inventoried and stored on the premises.

The mining activities of the French continued for five years, and each year their hoard grew and accumulated at the headquarters. Satisfied with the amount of gold they now possessed, the Frenchmen made plans to work for a few more months and then transport the bullion back to

New Orleans and thence to their homeland. Excited at the prospect of returning to France as wealthy men, the miners were unprepared for the misfortune that awaited them.

During the time the French were mining gold in the San Juan Mountains, two things occurred which were to spell doom for their operation. The first was the fact that increased mining activity by Spaniards was going on nearby, and they considered this region to be their own and resented the intrusion of others. The second had to do with the members of the French party. After working in the mines for as much as thirty and forty days at a stretch, the miners were often allowed to travel southeast to Santa Fe, where they relaxed and enjoyed the charms of the many young Spanish women who resided there. Some of the miners talked too freely to the young ladies about the great wealth being excavated from the rock in the San Juan Mountains. The *señoritas* eventually informed the Spanish miners and soldiers who also frequented this bustling city. Curious, the Spaniards investigated and learned the extent of the French mining operations. Once this information was reported to the Spanish authorities, plans were formed to rid the mountains of the French interlopers.

To accomplish this, the Spaniards recruited the local Indians and promised them a bounty on every French scalp that was brought to them. Soon Indian attacks on the French settlement became frequent, and during the next few months the force of three hundred men dwindled to less than a hundred. Hunting game to provide food for the miners also became hazardous because the hunters were often ambushed and killed. Provisions soon ran low and the Frenchmen found themselves in a desperate situation.

Realizing that to remain in the area would mean death to all, the leader of the miners decided to hide the accumulated gold, abandon the area temporarily, and return some time later to retrieve it, when the threat of Indians and Spaniards was not so great.

Before their departure, they hid the gold in one of the mine shafts located near the headquarters. This shaft was the most recently excavated and had a vertical opening some thirty feet deep before leveling off for another fifty feet or so into solid bedrock. Prior to receiving the gold, the shaft was reinforced with timbers and flat stone slabs. After hundreds of ingots had been carried into and stacked within the horizontal tunnel, the vertical portion of the shaft was filled with rock, dirt, and forest debris. Several marks indicting the location of the shaft were chiseled on nearby rocks and slashed on the trunks of trees.

By the time the gold had been hidden, the force of Frenchmen had dwindled to approximately thirty men. These few hardy souls, lacking provisions, fled from the area and headed eastward. After months of traveling, lost, hungry, and constantly menaced by hostile Indians, only two survived the ordeal and eventually arrived at a small settlement on the Missouri River near Kansas City. Within a few days, one of the Frenchmen died, but the other, a miner named Labreau, eventually made his way back to France. With him he carried a map to the hidden treasure in the San Juan Mountains, an incredible cache of gold estimated to be worth fifty million dollars!

On arriving in France, Labreau, unsure of what to do, delivered the map to French authorities. The chart, scratched onto the back of a tanned deerskin, provided precise directions to the treasure hoard on what has come to be known Treasure Mountain.

Time passed, Labreau died, and the map was set aside and forgotten until 1844, when another Frenchman found it. Excited at the possibility of recovering this tremendous cache of gold in the faraway Americas, he organized another party to journey to Colorado to try to find it.

Upon their arrival in Taos, New Mexico, the treasure hunters employed the services of a guide, a competent young Mexican named Bernardo Sanchez. With the explicit directions provided on the map and the capable leadership of Sanchez, the Frenchmen arrived without incident at the general location of the mines worked by the earlier party.

Unable to locate the huge cache, the Frenchmen did manage to find more gold ore in the abandoned shafts and in the local stream beds. For several weeks they mined and panned the ore, but were eventually chased from the area by hostile Indians.

When the Frenchmen returned to Taos, they allowed Sanchez to examine the old map closely and the Mexican guide discovered something that the others had missed. He interpreted some of the cryptic graphics on the old deerskin to mean that at a certain hour of a certain day during a specific month, a shadow cast by one of three large spruce trees passed directly over the shaft which held the buried treasure. At the center of the three spruce trees, equidistant from each, was a phony grave.

Sanchez explained his revelation to the Frenchmen, but the Europeans feared the Indians so much they refused to venture back to the San Juan Mountains and eventually returned to their native country, taking the map with them. Sanchez, relying on his memory, decided to wait for a few years and return to try to find the treasure on his own. At sixty years of age, however, his health began to fail him and he grew too infirm to make such an arduous journey. As time passed, he eventually forgot the pertinent timing relative to the casting of the shadow by the certain tree.

Several years later, an American explorer named Asa Poor, who was familiar with the tale of the buried French gold, located the mock grave. The spruce trees, however, were not to be found, and Poor believed they had simply died, fallen, and rotted away in the intervening years. Poor remained convinced that the treasure shaft was located somewhere close to the grave but was unable to find any evidence of it. Undoubtedly, in the time that had passed since the shaft was covered up, this part of the forest floor had come to look like any other.

50

Today, many people who are intimate with the story of the nearly fifty million dollars' worth of gold hidden in the San Juans know the location of Treasure Mountain and the mesa-like southern extension. Somewhere on that mesa, covered by several inches of soil, is the filled entrance to an abandoned mine shaft that contains one of the most incredible buried treasures ever hidden in America.

The Treasure of Deadman Cave

The three prospectors in the Sangre de Cristo Mountains were unprepared for the sudden blinding snowstorm and accompanying frigid weather, but the harsh conditions provided them with an opportunity that eventually led to the discovery of an uncommonly large cache of Spanish-smelted gold bars in a remote cave. With the exception of the three ingots removed by the trio, the treasure remains intact to this day, but its location has become a mystery.

Southern Colorado residents S.J. Harkman, H.A. Melton, and E.R. Oliver occasionally visited portions of the Sangre de Cristo range in south-central Colorado to prospect for gold and silver. Though they never recovered much ore, the three friends came to enjoy the weekends in the cool, clean air of this part of the Rocky Mountain chain, and they returned to their homes in Silver Cliff refreshed and rejuvenated as a result of their experiences.

On one memorable trip, the three men were surprised by an unexpected snowstorm. Because they had hiked several miles into the southern part of the range near Blanca Peak, they decided to seek shelter in a remote canyon rather than attempt to return through the blizzard to the location where they had parked their vehicle. Locating a jutting ledge that provided some protection from the strong winds and whirling snow, they built a small fire and warmed themselves while waiting for the storm to abate.

During a lull in the storm, as they enjoyed the peace and quiet of their white solitude, Harkman noticed an opening to a cave on the far wall of the canyon. With nothing better to do, the three friends crossed the canyon floor, climbed the gentle slope leading to the cave opening, and peered in.

Oliver crawled into the low, narrow passageway for about twelve feet and reported that it opened into a small chamber, just barely large enough to allow him to stand. From where he stood in the chamber, Oliver could barely discern the opening to another passageway at the far end. Deciding it might be fun to explore the cave, the three men gathered dry grasses and sticks of pine with which to fashion crude torches and, together, entered the cave.

The second passageway proved to be no longer than the first. At the end, however, it opened into a much larger room. Even with the three men holding torches in the center of the chamber, they were unable to see the adjacent walls. Slowly and carefully, the men began to explore around this room, when Melton struck his foot against a dust-covered object. Lowering his torch, he drew back in surprise as he gazed upon a human skull.

Realizing the cave held more promise than they initially believed, the three ventured outside, gathered armloads of dry wood, and returned to the second chamber, where they built a large fire in the center. With greater illumination, the three were able to explore the room more effectively. During the next twenty minutes, five more skeletons were discovered. In addition to these grisly prizes, another passageway was found.

Carrying torches, the three prospectors entered this narrow but longer passage, crawling on their hands and knees. After traversing a difficult sixty feet, they found that this tube-like extension opened into yet a third chamber somewhat smaller than the first. As the men, now rather tired, rested on the rock and dirt floor, they noticed an irregular pattern along the far wall. Crawling over to it, Oliver held his torch high and gazed upon what he thought were rocks stacked against the wall. He picked one up and was immediately surprised at its great weight. After looking at it closely, Oliver realized it was a gold ingot and called for his companions. With all three men holding their torches over the huge stack of gold bars, Melton counted over four hundred of them. The thick layer of dust atop the stack suggested the bars had reposed there for many years, perhaps even centuries.

As the men sat in the cave, marveling at their discovery, they noticed two more passageways extending from this third chamber, passageways they believed might hold more gold ingots. Because their torches were burning low, however, they abandoned their plans to explore them and decided instead to leave the cavern.

With each man pushing one of the heavy ingots before him, they eventually exited the cave. Later that afternoon, when the intensity of the storm had lessened somewhat, they made their way down the trail to the vehicle and returned home to Silver Cliff. Here they had the gold bars analyzed, and discovered each was worth nine hundred dollars! In addition, each of the ingots had imprinted on its surface a symbol which suggested they were of Spanish origin. History is replete with references to Spanish occupation and mining in this region since the sixteenth century, and it was concluded that the large cache was associated with events of that era.

After exchanging the gold bars for cash, the three friends decided they would return to the Sangre de Cristo Mountains to retrieve the remaining ingots and live the rest of their lives in luxurious wealth. The worst part of winter had already set in, however, and plans were delayed until the spring thaw, when negotiating the rugged and sometimes dangerous mountain trails would be easier.

When spring finally arrived, the three made preparations to return to Deadman Cave—as they referred to the cavern because of the presence of the skeletons—and gather their fortune. On arriving back in the approximate area of the canyon in which they had first encountered the snowstorm of several weeks earlier, the three men became confused and disoriented, and disagreed on directions and distance. For several days they combed the region in search of the cave that held the incredible fortune in gold ingots, but gradually grew frustrated when every place they searched bore little or no resemblance to the canyon as they remembered it.

After several weekends of searching the area for the elusive cavern and not finding it, the men finally gave up. They concluded that, because of the reduced visibility created by the snowstorm and the fact that a deep layer of snow had covered much of the canyon floor, they would be unable to recognize the exact location of the cave on return expeditions.

Although many suspected Harkman, Melton, and Oliver of fabricating the entire tale of the cave and the treasure cache, the three men have remained unshakable in their insistence that both are real, and several witnesses have seen the three gold ingots the men removed from the the cave.

Whoever might be lucky enough to find Deadman Cave and the hundreds of gold ingots stacked within will come into possession of a fortune in gold unheard of in modern times.

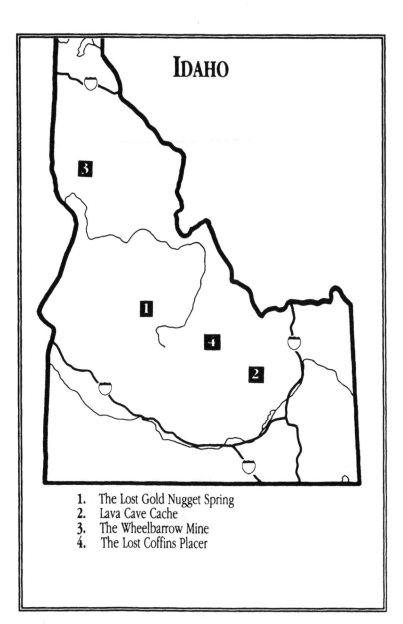

IDAHO

1. The Lost Gold Nugget Spring
2. Lava Cave Cache
3. The Wheelbarrow Mine
4. The Lost Coffins Placer

The Lost Gold Nugget Spring

More than a hundred years ago, a prospector and his son accidentally discovered one of the most unusual deposits on the North American continent, a deposit that apparently yielded a large fortune but which has since become lost. Because of the sudden and unexpected death of his son, the prospector was forced to abandon the site. He was never able to return. Only one other man knew the location of the gold, but misfortune also struck him and he was unable to retrieve any of it. Since that time the secret location has been found at least once. It may be just a matter of time before this rich deposit of gold is rediscovered.

For two years during the second half of the 1880s, a man named Charles Curtiss, accompanied by his young son, packed into and explored the mountain ranges of central Idaho in search of gold. Now and then they would select a likely stream, set up a temporary camp, and pan for gold. More often than not they encountered only disappointment, but each of them held tightly to the belief that someday their fortunes would change and they would strike it rich.

One day, Curtiss and his son rode into a level meadow near an old trail that was often used to transport equipment from Missoula, Montana, to the gold miners near Boise. The meadow, between five and ten acres in size, was covered with rich and nutritious grasses on which Curtiss loosed his eight horses to graze. Deciding to settle at this location, father and son constructed a crude, two-room log cabin with a rock fireplace and chimney. Clear, fresh drinking water was drawn from a nearby spring.

Area prospectors and miners who knew Curtiss often wondered out loud why he decided to give up prospecting activities and take up homesteading. Curtiss had a reputation among his peers as a dedicated gold-seeker who had chased his fortune for years, and his friends grew curious when he suddenly chose to settle down.

Curtiss never explained his actions to anyone, preferring to remain in relative solitude in the remote high country meadow with his son. Every few weeks, the two made trips to Boise to purchase supplies and furnishings for the cabin. On each occasion, Curtiss paid for his goods with nuggets of pure gold. Because Curtiss had never announced a gold strike, his friends were at a loss to explain his newfound wealth.

During the severe winter of 1890, Curtiss's son came down with a high fever and delirium. Fearing the worst, Curtiss left the boy in the cabin and went for help. The deep snowdrifts impeded his progress getting down off the mountain, but just when he was about to give up, Curtiss encountered an Indian living alone in a dugout off to one side of the trail. Curtiss begged the Indian to go to Boise, about a hundred miles away, and try to find a doctor for his son. The Indian, whose name was Siawhia, agreed to go for help, and Curtiss returned to his cabin.

Five days later Siawhia appeared at Curtiss's cabin, alone. He handed Curtis a bottle of dark-colored liquid and explained to him that the doctor could not come to the mountains but had sent some medicine instead. For two days, Curtiss and Siawhia nursed the youngster and gave him the medicine, but despite their efforts the boy died.

The following morning Curtiss and Siawhia buried the boy behind the cabin and piled a mound of rocks approximately four feet high over the grave. Tearfully, Curtiss bowed his head and recited a prayer.

The next day, Curtiss told Siawhia he was going to travel to California to inform his wife of the death of their son. He explained to the Indian that, while living at the meadow, he and his son had discovered a rich deposit of gold nearby, and he would be returning to this site with his wife to continue to mine it. He asked Siawhia if he would remain at the cabin and take care of the horses while he was gone. He cautioned the Indian to make certain no one disturbed the spring in his absence, since it was the only source of water for miles around.

While he was packing to leave, Curtiss removed five ore sacks from behind a loose rock in the fireplace. Opening one of them, he spilled the contents onto the table to show the Indian, and Siawhia stared in amazement at the bright shiny nuggets of pure gold. Curtiss told the Indian that the nuggets were so abundant at his secret location, they could be easily scooped up by hand. As he bade Siawhia goodbye, Curtiss told the Indian that on his return he would pay him well for minding the place and would bring him a new rifle as a gift. From the doorway of the cabin, Siawhia watched Curtiss ride his horse out into the snow and onto the trail that led to Boise.

For weeks, Siawhia remained at the cabin, caring for the horses and maintaining Curtiss's property. When he ran low on supplies, the Indian would ride to the nearest mining camp and stock up, using a small amount of gold Curtiss had left for that purpose.

About ten weeks following the departure of Curtiss, the skies cleared, the temperatures rose, and the snow began to slowly melt from this high-altitude location. Until this time, Siawhia had merely gathered and melted snow when he needed drinking water, but now that the snow was gone he knew he must rely on the spring.

On the morning when Siawhia arrived at the spring for the first time, he discovered it was clogged with fallen leaves, pine needles, and branches. Taking Curtiss's shovel he began to clean it out when he made a startling discovery. Once the debris had been removed and the clear cold water flowed freely into the small depression, Siawhia noticed that the bottom of the pool was covered with pea-sized gold nuggets! The Indian suddenly realized this was where Curtiss obtained his gold.

Excitedly, Siawhia scooped two large handfuls of gold from the bottom of the shallow pool and filled his pockets. Realizing what a fortune such as this would buy him, he locked up the cabin and rode directly to Boise. On arriving in the bustling mining town, Siawhia went to the nearest tavern and proceeded to get quite drunk. All night long he consumed liquor until he finally passed out. Several of the bar patrons, believing the Indian to be seriously ill, carried him to the office of the town physician.

The next morning Siawhia awoke in the doctor's office. His head throbbed maddeningly as a result of the alcohol from the night before, but something far more serious was troubling him. Siawhia suddenly realized he could not see anything—he was blind! The doctor was at a loss to explain this, but suggested it might be due to some impurities in the great quantity of liquor the Indian had consumed the previous night.

Eventually Siawhia returned to the small town of Burgdorf near the Salmon River Mountains. Here he lived out the remainder of his life in a run-down shack with a dirt floor and little in the way of furnishings. For a time he survived thanks to donations from friendly residents of Burgdorf, and then the county welfare agency provided needed assistance.

As far as Siawhia knew, Curtiss never returned to the Salmon River Mountains. Many nights as the old Indian lay in his cot he dreamed of the gold nuggets shining from the bottom of the little pool of clear water by the spring. If he could only see, thought Siawhia, he would return to the meadow, retrieve the gold, and become a rich man.

In 1960, a part-time prospector named Rhea was exploring the area in and around the Salmon River Mountains by car, when he chanced to stop at a small mercantile to purchase some needed supplies. On his way into the store, Rhea spotted an old, blind Indian carrying a small sack of food and attempting to step down off the high wooden porch. Rushing to the old man's aid, Rhea gave him his arm and gently helped him down the steps.

The Indian offered his thanks and introduced himself as Siawhia. He told Rhea that he came to this place to purchase food once a week from his residence about a mile away. Rhea told Siawhia that if he would wait a few minutes while he purchased some supplies, he would give him a ride to his home.

As the two rode slowly down the blacktop, Rhea told Siawhia that he was prospecting for gold in the nearby mountains. Siawhia sat quiety for a few minutes, and then launched into the story of the gold-filled spring of Charles Curtiss.

Rhea listened intently as the old man relived that winter so many years ago in the mountains. When the Indian finished, Rhea asked him if he would like to accompany him to the mountains in an attempt to relocate the spring. Siawhia, although he was over ninety years of age, readily agreed and looked forward to the adventure.

The next morning, Rhea picked up Siawhia at his residence and they drove into the mountains. Relying purely on the old man's memory, Rhea steered his vehicle onto numerous twisting dirt roads. As he described the landscape to the Indian, Siawhia would smile and say he remembered, and then provide Rhea with more directions.

Eventually they reached a point where the road ended. Siawhia gave Rhea a set of directions from that point which would take him two to three miles deeper into the hills. That afternoon, Rhea took Siawhia back to his residence and thanked him for his help.

Early the next morning, Rhea drove back to the location where the road ended and, following the old Indian's instructions, hiked into the woods. Presently he came to an old trail, just as the Indian had said he would, and followed it for nearly half an hour until he arrived at a meadow.

Believing this to be the meadow on which Curtiss and his son settled, Rhea spent the next hour searching for the old cabin, but was unable to find anything resembling such a structure. Just as he was about to give up, he located it. The old log cabin had fallen over and was covered with grass, weeds, and forest debris. Nearby, Rhea found the remains of a shed and a pole corral where Curtiss had kept his horses.

Continuing his search of the area, Rhea soon discovered the grave of the younger Curtiss, a large mound of rock, partially sunk into the soft meadow ground.

Convinced he was at the correct location, Rhea undertook to search for the spring. Examining the area closely, it was clear that the spring had apparently dried up long ago. So much grass, shrub, and timber had grown up in the meadow since Siawhia's departure many years earlier that locating the feature was going to prove difficult.

Although he searched all day long, Rhea was unable to find the spring. With the day almost over the temperature began to drop sharply, and he decided to return to his vehicle.

Due to his job commitments, Rhea found it necessary to return home the next day. When he did, he discovered he had been offered a new position in Alaska. Because he had a wife and children, he opted to take the job and moved shortly thereafter, abandoning his plans to return to the Salmon River Mountains.

Siawhia passed away around 1970 at approximately one hundred years of age. The location of Charles Curtiss's gold-filled spring in the Salmon River Mountains remains a mystery to this day.

Lava Cave Cache

The stagecoach rumbled and bounced along the hard, winding,narrow trail through the lava beds. The coach was not making very good time—the day was hot, the horses were tired, and the load was heavier than usual with four passengers and two 125-pound gold bars wrapped in canvas and tied to the top.

On the previous day, the driver and his companion had loaded the heavy bars onto the roof of the coach when they stopped at the Custer Mine near the headwaters of Big Lost River. Because the mining company had been plagued by frequent stagecoach robberies, they had taken to casting oversized bars in the hope that the greater weight would discourage future attempts. The time period was the mid-1880s, and highwaymen were taking a severe toll on the Custer Mine's profits. In the event that robbers did seize the gold, the heavier weight would slow them down so that capture and recovery would be easier.

The driver pulled the coach to a stop near Big Southern Butte, a volcanic landform rising more than two thousand feet from the plains near the periphery of an extensive lava bed lying to the west. After watering the horses at a nearby spring and allowing the passengers to stretch their legs, the signal was given to load up and proceed toward the town of Blackfoot, located about another thirty miles to the southeast.

The stagecoach route followed an old trail that wound through several arms of the lava beds. On occasion, the horses were slowed to a walk as the driver negotiated numerous difficult passages through the low, narrow canyons. Some of the passes were so constricted that the passengers could reach out the windows of the coach and touch the rough lava walls.

It was in one such location that a barricade of large rocks had been thrown across the trail. Just as the driver pulled the horses to a halt, a masked gunman stepped out from behind a niche in the lava wall and leveled a shotgun at the driver and his helper. After having them give up their pistols, the gunman ordered the two men to untie the gold bars and throw them to the ground. Once that was done, the bandit relieved the passengers of their valuables. Within minutes, the road was cleared and the coach was sent on its way.

As soon as the stage was out of sight, the bandit lifted one of the heavy gold bars and, with great difficulty, carried it to a small cave in the lava rock a short distance away. After a brief rest, he returned for the other bar. With the gold lying just inside the shallow cave he had picked out earlier in the day, the bandit then covered the small opening with branches and rocks.

When the coach arrived in Blackfoot, the driver alerted the sheriff and a posse was soon assembled. Returning to the site of the holdup, they immediately picked up the outlaw's trail at a point only a few dozen yards from the gold bars reposing in the shallow cave.

After four days of tenacious tracking northward, the posse arrived at the town of Salmon near the Montana border. Upon questioning several residents about newcomers to the town, they were directed to a tavern where they found a man spending money quite freely. The man matched the description provided by the stagecoach driver, and was in possession of valuables that belonged to some of the passengers. He was immediately arrested.

After lengthy questioning, the man finally admitted to robbing the stagecoach. He told the law officers about how he had hidden the gold in the lava cave, and offered to return to the area and show them. During the ride back to the lava beds, the good-natured prisoner cooperated completely, even engaging in occasional conversation and joking with the posse members.

Nightfall was approaching as the party neared the holdup site. The sheriff suggested they stop for the night and undertake a search to retrieve the gold in the morning. As the party sat around the campfire that evening eating beans and drinking coffee, the prisoner told them how, before fleeing the site, he had set up three locational markers to help him find the gold when he returned. Near the center of the three markers, he explained, was the cave.

Following breakfast the next morning, the prisoner and posse mounted up and rode toward the area of the cave. Almost immediately, the bandit rode up to the first marker and pointed it out to the lawmen. Scanning the area from his position in the saddle, he appeared to be slightly confused. He pointed toward the east and told the deputies that be thought one of the markers lay in that direction. Then looking toward the west, he suggested another might be over there. About half of the posse members rode east and the other half, accompanied by the prisoner, rode west.

As the prisoner and three of the deputies slowly rode across the hot lava beds, they gradually became separated by short distances. During the past few days, the lawmen had become comfortable with their captive and felt he could be trusted. As the distance between the men increased, the prisoner casually steered his mount to a low ridge, crossed it, and descended to the other side. Once out of sight of the lawmen, he spurred his horse and fled from the area. It was the last time they ever saw him. Although they searched the region for the rest of the day, the lawmen could find neither the other two markers nor the cave which contained the gold.

Thirty years later, a stranger appeared in the town of Arco, located along the old stagecoach route between Challis and Blackfoot. The stranger would occasionally disappear into the lava beds for days at a time and then suddenly reappear in town. About two months after the stranger arrived, he took into his confidence one of the Arco residents and told him a strange tale. He said that several months earlier, he had met a man in New Mexico who told him about robbing a stagecoach of two large gold bars and hiding them inside a small cave in the nearby lava beds. For reasons unexplained by the stranger, the robber was unable to return to the area, but he provided a map purporting to show the location of the hidden cache.

The map clearly depicted the lava beds, Big Southern Butte, the old stagecoach trail, and the cache. When the stranger arrived at the site of the thirty-year-old robbery, he was surprised to discover dozens of caves such as the one described on the map. Although he searched every one of them, he was never able to find the gold bars. At least that is what he told everyone in Arco.

One day, however, the stranger simply disappeared. Many guessed he had finally located the gold and fled with it. Others claimed he grew discouraged with the search and abandoned the region.

If, in fact, the gold bars are still lying in a shallow rocky cave along the old stagecoach route—and many believe they are—their value today would be approximately a hundred thousand dollars.

The Wheelbarrow Mine

During the summer of 1880, a prospector known only as Caspar, along with his partner, roamed the wilds of the Moscow Mountains in northern Idaho in search of gold. Caspar had been a hard-luck case for most of his life, always searching but never finding anything of value. Unable to read or write, always dressed in little more than rags and leading an emaciated mule, Caspar was often the brunt of jokes and derision. Although some would occasionally grubstake the down-and-out Caspar, most avoided him and none ever truly believed he was intelligent enough to recognize gold if he saw it.

But recognize it he did, for one afternoon while examining a promising outcrop along a sloping canyon wall, Caspar discovered a thick vein of quartz richly laced with gold. He and his partner immediately set up a camp, and the next day they were busy extracting the ore and tunneling into the hillside following the rich vein.

Several weeks passed, and the two men made excellent progress. The tunnel extended deep into the hillside and the gold continued to accumulate. While one of the men dug in the tunnel, the other would load the rock and ore into a homemade wheelbarrow and transport it to a location several yards beyond the entrance, where it was dumped. The wheelbarrow was fashioned from the staves of a whiskey barrel, some hand-cut poles, and an old, rusted metal wheel.

As winter approached, Caspar's partner suggested they abandon the high mountains before the cold weather set in and the heavy snows fell. He felt they had accumulated enough gold to make them rich, and he did not relish the prospect of more hard labor in the mine during the bitterly cold months ahead.

Caspar, on the other hand, insisted they remain and dig as much gold as they could. He also expressed a fear that if they abandoned the area others might move in and take over the mine.

The discussion about whether to leave or to stay soon grew into a bitter argument, and before it could be resolved Caspar, in a fit of rage, killed his partner with a crushing blow to the head with a hammer. Panicked, Caspar then loaded the body into the wheelbarrow and rolled it into the deepest part of the mine.

Afraid of being caught and punished for murder, Caspar loaded what gold he could into saddlebags and fled. Several weeks later, he arrived in Sacramento, where he lived well for many years on his gold.

Approximately twenty years later, Caspar ran low on funds and decided to return to his rich gold mine in the Moscow Mountains to dig for more gold. Arriving in Troy, Idaho, he convinced a man named William McGahan to go into partnership with him, and soon the two were riding into the mountains in search of the mine.

Once in the mountains, however, Caspar became disoriented and recognized very little of the area he once knew so intimately. Time and again he became lost and, dejected, he eventually gave up the search and returned to California. McGahan, who kept a diary, wrote down the story of Caspar and the lost mine.

In 1940, Dr. C.L. Treichler, a resident of Palouse, Washington, came into possession of McGahan's journal and found the story of Caspar and the lost mine. Palouse is near the Idaho border, not far from the Moscow Mountains and the area where Caspar's mine was allegedly located. Because Treichler was a prominent investor in several productive gold mines in the area, he was aware of the great potential for finding valuable ore in these mountains. Intrigued with McGahan's account, Treichler found credibility in Caspar's story and decided to try to locate the old mine.

At every opportunity, Treichler searched the area described in the journal, hoping someday to make a lucky discovery. And one day it happened. On a heavily timbered canyon slope he found a pile of mine tailings grown over with thick brush and young trees. Not far away was the caved-in entrance to a tunnel.

Employing experienced miner Jack Moore of Potlach, Idaho, Treichler had the cave-in debris removed. Once they were able to enter the mine, Treichler and Moore lit lanterns and cautiously explored the old tunnel, fearful of the unsupported and loosely consolidated rock. Approximately forty feet from the entrance, their lanterns illuminated an old, crudely fashioned wheelbarrow. On closer inspection, the two men discovered the grisly, mummified corpse of Caspar's murdered partner.

Stepping beyond the wheelbarrow, Treichler inspected a likely-looking vein against the far wall and was elated to discover a thick seam of gold-bearing quartz. He and Moore filled several ore pouches with the ore and sent it to Walla Walla, Washington, for assay. A few days later, Treichler received word that his sample was incredibly rich.

Treichler and Moore made plans to return to the location of the old mine and continue to excavate it, following the vein. After several weeks of preparation, the two men finally arrived at the site only to find that another cave-in had occurred, almost completely filling the shaft. The rich seam of ore was now separated from the miners by thousands of tons of rock.

For several days the two men worked to remove the debris. After approximately ten feet of shaft had been cleared, another cave-in occurred, refilling it completely.

Undeterred, Treichler decided to excavate a second shaft that would intersect the vein of gold deep in the mountain, but after experiencing several more cave-ins and problems with ground water gushing into the tunnel, he finally gave up.

Since Treichler abandoned the area, no one has returned to this part of the Moscow Mountains in an attempt to reopen what is known locally as the Wheelbarrow Mine. Because there are no roads into this area, heavy excavating equipment cannot be brought to the site, so if the mine is reopened it must be done carefully by hand and with dynamite, with the risk of cave-in a serious possibility at all times.

If, however, the shaft can be reopened and shored up appropriately, an incredible fortune in gold awaits the determined miner who is willing to take the chance.

The Lost Coffins Placer

James L. Jerome was a well-known and well-liked businessman in southeastern Idaho during the early part of the twentieth century. Residing in Pocatello the last thirty years of his life, he was a mainstay of the community, raised a fine family, and was generally regarded by all as a decent man and good neighbor. When he was much younger, Jerome found what may have been one of the richest placer mines in the history of the United States. Within only a few hours after panning an impressive amount of gold from the deposit, Jerome, running from bushwhackers, watched the entire upper end of the small valley that contained the placer mine become buried by a huge rock slide.

As a young man, James Jerome had spent a great deal of time prospecting for gold among the numeorus promising rock outcrops encountered in the Lost River Range north of the town of Mackay. From time to time Jerome rode to the small settlement to stock up on provisions, visit with a few friends over a round of beers at a local tavern, and then return to the mountains.

During one trip to Mackay, Jerome met an old prospector named George Coffins. Coffins, instantly recognizable by his tattered overalls and the ever-present briar pipe dangling from his mouth, was well known in the area as an eccentric old-timer who poked around the small streams of the Lost River Range in search of substantial placer deposits. Though he received an occasional grubstake from local citizens, no one believed the old man had much of a chance of ever finding anything. On a warm July evening in 1894, however, Coffin entered the tavern, yelled to everyone that the drinks were on him, and poured about five pounds of gold nuggets onto the bar from a canvas ore sack.

All through the evening, Coffins and the tavern patrons celebrated the old man's good fortune. Finally, around two in the morning, the prospector decided it was time to ride to the creek near the edge of town where he customarily set up camp. Jerome, who was also camped at the small creek, offered to ride back with Coffins.

Once in camp, the two men sat around a campfire discussing their prospecting and mining experiences in the nearby mountains. At one point Coffins asked Jerome if he would like to go into partnership with him on his placer mine. Coffins told the young man that it was the richest placer deposit he had ever seen and likely held enough gold to make a hundred men wealthy. Jerome enthusiastically agreed, and Coffins spent the next hour telling him about the placer and its location.

The next morning when Jerome woke up and stirred the fire, he observed Coffins packing some gear he had purchased in town the previous day. As he prepared some packs for lashing onto his burros, the old man set two cans of blasting powder nearby. Hefting one of the cans, Coffins commented that it felt light and said he was going to open it to see if it was full. With his lighted pipe dangling from his mouth, he pried the lid off the can. Almost instantly, the campsite was rocked by a tremendous explosion. Apparently, a spark from Coffins's pipe ignited the powder, instantly killing him and a burro standing nearby, and knocking Jerome to the ground.

Over the next two days, Jerome made arrangements for Coffins's funeral and contacted his relatives. With approval from the sheriff, Jerome sold Coffins's two remaining burros and equipment, converted the two pouches of gold found in his saddlebags into cash, and sent the entire amount to a daughter in Pennsylvania.

This done, Jerome decided to ride into the mountains and try to locate Coffins's rich placer using the directions the dead man had provided two nights earlier.

For several days, Jerome roamed the high country, following a series of canyons in search of the placer. Several times during his journey, Jerome had the feeling he was being followed, but each time he scanned the trail behind him he saw nothing.

On the evening of the fifth day, while Jerome was squatting near his campfire, a shot rang out from behind some trees about fifty yards away. As bullets whistled by him, Jerome grabbed his rifle, dove for cover, and fired several shots into the darkness. A few minutes of quiet followed, which were suddenly broken by a voice in the distance. The speaker informed Jerome that there were five men hiding in the trees and that they knew he was searching for Coffins's placer mine. The voice insisted Jerome throw in with them and share the wealth. Jerome, afraid the men intended to kill him after locating the placer, said he was simply riding to his own diggings and didn't know anything about Coffins's secret location.

When the voice became insistent, Jerome fired his rifle in the direction from which it came, and for the next fifteen minutes he exchanged shots with the men hiding in the trees. From the sounds he heard in he dark, he believed he had killed one of them and badly wounded another. Presently the shooting stopped and Jerome could hear the men riding away.

Remaining hidden throughout the night, Jerome emerged only after the sun had risen and illuminated the landscape. Inspecting the place in the trees from which the shots had been fired the previous night, he found several pools of congealed blood, proof that he had indeed hit one or more of his attackers.

Following a quick breakfast, Jerome hurriedly loaded his burros and, believing his trackers had abandoned the chase, continued to search for Coffins's placer mine.

Proceeding up a narrow canyon which contained the headwaters of a small tributary, Jerome was almost near the end of it when he found evidence of an abandoned campsite. Searching around, he discovered a primitive metal and wood gold rocker used to wash the nuggets from the stream debris. Jerome realized he had finally found Coffins's secret location. Carrying his pan, he walked over to the small stream, scooped some gravel into it, and swirled it around for several seconds. Almost immediately, Jerome was rewarded with the glimmer of gold in the bottom of the pan.

After looking about the area and assuring himself he had not been followed, Jerome unpacked his burros and set up a small tent. Exploring along the walls of the narrow canyon, he found a cache of tools stuffed into a niche located at ground level. Among the tools were two cans of blasting powder.

For the rest of the afternoon, Jerome washed stream gravel in his pan and collected nearly a pound and a half of sizeable gold nuggets. For two more days he panned gold, eventually filling three ore sacks with the fine, pure ore. After panning at several locations along the little stream, Jerome became convinced that this placer was incredibly rich, for sizeable nuggets lay visible in the gravel virtually everywhere he looked.

During the afternoon of his third day in the canyon, Jerome decided to ride to a lower elevation and hunt for deer, as he was in need of meat.

Within an hour Jerome located and shot a young doe. After cutting the backstraps and haunches from the animal, he tied the meat onto his horse and proceeded back to the diggings. On the return trip, Jerome noticed some fresh tracks on the trail he had ridden down an hour earlier.

At least three horsemen had recently passed this way and were apparently headed toward the placer mine.

On returning to his campsite, Jerome cautiously looked about but could find no evidence that anyone was nearby. Satisfied he was alone, he wrapped the fresh meat in some canvas and went to the stream to pan for more gold. The third time he dipped his pan into the cold water, several shots rang out from behind a row of boulders near the canyon wall, where the tools and blasting powder were located. Rushing to his campsite, Jerome picked up his rifle and took cover behind a fallen log several yards away.

After about ten minutes of exchanging gunfire, Jerome realized he was at a disadvantage and looked for a way to escape. Firing several shots at the intruders, he quickly scurried to the shelter of a large pine tree located about fifteen yards to the rear. By pacing his retreat in this manner, he managed to put significant distance between him and his attackers over the next twenty minutes.

Jerome decided to fire his remaining shells at the men behind the boulders and then flee down the canyon in an attempt to get away. One of his bullets ricocheted off a rock and plowed into a can of blasting powder lying only a few feet from the aggressors. Instantly a huge explosion rocked the upper end of the canyon and tons of overhanging rock fell down upon the attackers, covering them completely. Within just a few seconds, a second and larger rock slide occurred, and Jerome watched in fascination as a large part of the canyon wall slid and tumbled into the narrow valley, completely burying his camp and the gold-filled stream under several feet of rock.

Jerome turned and fled on foot, not stopping until he was nearly four miles from the narrow canyon. A few days later, Jerome arrived at Mackay, where he told his story.

Though he continued to prospect in and around the Lost River Range for the next few years, James Jerome never returned to the location of Coffins's placer mine. Before he died in 1938, he told others of his story and attempted to draw maps of and provide directions to the small canyon, but the years had dimmed his memory. Today, in some narrow, remote canyon deep in the Lost River Range, a phenomenally rich placer mine, along with three skeletons, lies under several feet of rock debris. Had Jerome not been determined to escape from his attackers by retreating down the canyon, he might very well have perished, and the story of Coffins's placer would never have been told.

MONTANA

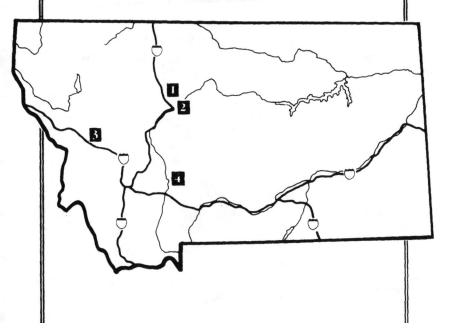

1. Lost Train Robbery Gold
2. Henry Plummer's Lost Gold
3. Outlaw Skinner's Buried Gold
4. Springer's Lost Load

Lost Train Robbery Gold

The five masked men nervously awaited the arrival of the St. Paul, Minneapolis, and Manitoba Railroad train as it cautiously rolled along the newly laid tracks. The men, on horseback behind a covering of trees and boulders, were ordinary cowhands who had decided to rob a train for lack of anything better to do. Little did they know they would soon come into possession of an incredible fortune in gold coins and ingots.

During the fall of 1887, Clem Durkel and four friends were playing cards in the bunkhouse of the D.H.S. Cattle Ranch in Judith Basin, Montana. Roundup had been completed two weeks earlier and the men found themselves with nothing to do until spring. Poker was growing boring, and they had spent most of their wages on a few reckless nights in town several days earlier. The tedium of waiting around the D.H.S. Ranch for three more months grated on the nerves of the idle cowhands as they tried to come up with some form of diversion.

One evening while all five were seated in front of the bunkhouse, Durkel suggested they rob a train. The idea appealed to the others, and soon plans were being made to hold up the SP, M, & M as it made its way northward on the brand new railroad bed from the town of Great Falls.

In order to avoid suspicion, the cowhands left the D.H.S. Ranch one at a time over the next few days. Finally meeting at a predesignated point outside of Great Falls, they rode alongside the railroad tracks one afternoon, searching for an ideal location from which to pull off the robbery. They settled on a site about eighteen miles north of Great Falls.

The would-be train robbers expected to gain little from the holdup save some amusement for themselves. Everyone knew the SP, M, & M carried nothing but mail and freight. On this cold day in late November, however, the train was hauling an unanticipated shipment of fifty thousand dollars in gold coins along with twenty-five gold ingots. It was estimated that the total value of the golden cargo was about two hundred thousand dollars.

Because the railroad track had been completed only a few weeks earlier, the engineer guided the train along slowly and cautiously, keeping an eye out for uneven track. As the train crested a low rise, the engineer spotted several crossties piled on the tracks about a hundred yards distant. His first inclination was to ram the stack of ties and break through, but as the potential for derailment was high, he slowed the train to a halt and prepared to investigate.

Just as the train came to a stop, the five masked men charged from behind their cover, brandishing pistols. One of them leaped from his horse and into the cab of the locomotive. While he ordered the engineer and fireman to raise their hands, the other four rode to the express car and demanded it be unlocked. The frightened messenger slid the heavy door aside and stared into the barrels of four pistols.

When the bandits ordered the messenger to turn over anything of value, they were taken by surprise when he opened the safe and produced several canvas sacks filled with gold coins. While the outlaws marveled at their incredible luck, the messenger also showed them the twenty-five gold ingots!

Hastily, the outlaws stuffed coins and ingots into saddlebags and pockets, then ordered the train to proceeed as they rode away to the northeast.

About twenty minutes later, the train pulled into Fort Benton, where the engineer telegraphed the news of the robbery to the sheriff at Great Falls. The sheriff quickly gathered a posse, and loading men and horses onto the next train, rode it northward to the holdup scene.

The posse followed the tracks of the outlaws for about two miles to the northeast and found they had doubled back, crossed the tracks at a point only fifty yards south of the robbery scene, and proceeded toward the confluence of the Missouri and Sun Rivers. From here the bandits headed west toward the small settlement of Sun River, about twenty miles west of Great Falls.

The outlaws were having great difficulty transporting the heavy weight of so much gold, and their escape was slowed to a mere walk because of the burden. Arriving in Sun River, they attempted to trade for fresh mounts, but no one had any to spare.

Several of the Sun River residents noticed the look of desperation on the faces of the five men.

Realizing they needed to find a place to hide and rest their tired mounts, the train robbers rode out of Sun River and into a seldom-traveled portion of the east slope of the Rocky Mountains. They stopped near the base of Haystack Butte, built a small fire, and prepared a meal. With a freshwater spring nearby, the outlaws decided to rest at this location for two days, divide the gold, and be on their way. They believed they had eluded any pursuers and were confident that their holdup and getaway were a complete success. While the bandits sat around the campfire enjoying their evening meal and discussing what they would do with their newly acquired fortunes, the posse was questioning residents of Sun River.

Virtually everyone in the small community had seen the five men riding weary horses toting heavy packs. They quickly pointed out the direction they took on leaving town, and with no difficulty at all the sheriff and his men located and followed the tracks of the tired ponies through the night.

The following morning, just as the men were finishing breakfast, one of the outlaws walked over to the picket line to check on the horses. As he was looking after the mounts, he noticed a line of riders coming over a low ridge about three quarters of a mile to the southeast. At the head of the riders was a man who was obviously pointing out the tracks the five outlaws had left the previous evening.

Quickly saddling their horses and loading the gold into saddlebags, the bandits abandoned their gear and escaped into the nearby foothills.

After riding hard for about four miles, the horses grew exhausted from the weight of the gold. Now and again the outlaws could see the posse closing the distance. Realizing the need to lighten their load, the five decided to cache the gold, make their escape through the mountains, and return another day to retrieve it.

As they were searching for a suitable location in which to hide the loot, they arrived at a small mountain lake. Looking at the shimmering waters of the lake, Durkel had an idea which he quickly explained to his comrades. Following his lead, the bandits rode their horses into the shallow lake, pulled the sacks of coins and gold ingots out of their saddlebags, and dropped them into the cold waters. Relieved of their heavy burden, the bandits were able to make good time riding through the mountains.

When the posse arrived at the lake, they observed how the tracks of their quarry led into the water. Believing the bandits had only wished to water their horses, the pursuers continued on their way, oblivious to the fortune in gold only three feet below the surface of the lake.

The Durkel gang managed to elude the posse and escape into Idaho. Fearful of returning to the lake until things cooled off, the men separated, agreeing to meet in a year, return to the area, and recover the gold.

Several months later, two members of the gang decided that robbery was an easier way to make a living than working on a cattle ranch, so they tried to hold up a bank in Grangeville, Idaho. Both were killed during the attempt.

Another of the bandits murdered a man during an argument in a saloon in Lewiston and was sentenced to a life term in prison. The fourth bandit attempted to rob a stagecoach in California, was apprehended, tried, convicted, and sentenced to twenty years at hard labor. It is believed he died in prison.

Durkel, who had had his fill of the outlaw life, went to work on a cattle ranch in southern Idaho.

Three years after the train robbery, Durkel decided to return to the remote lake in the eastern foothills of the Montana Rockies near Sun River and retrieve the gold. Because there were no established trails into this unpopulated region, and because Durkel remembered little of the region and its landmarks from the time of his flight from the posse, he had difficulty getting his bearings and became lost several times.

Time after time Durkel traveled into the mountains near Haystack Butte in search of the gold-filled lake, and each time he was disappointed. Certain that incredible wealth still lay beneath the water of the elusive lake, he never gave up. By 1910, twenty-three years after the robbery, Durkel narrowed his search to two remote mountain lakes, one of which he was convinced must contain the gold.

As Durkel was growing older, out of a job, and running low on funds, he abandoned his search for a time to find work. He eventually secured employment with a man named Frank Bell, owner of a freight line that ran goods from Helena to the mining camps in the mountains. After Durkel had worked for Bell a year, he revealed to his employer the story of the train robbery and the fortune in gold lying in a lake somewhere in the mountains. Bell was fascinated and asked to become Durkel's partner.

Selecting one of the two lakes Durkel believed held the gold, the men set up a camp on its shore. For two full days they waded into the cold waters, searching and probing for the gold ingots and sacks of gold coins. The longer they remained in the area the more convinced Durkel became that this was indeed the lake in which they had dumped the loot. Unfortunately, nothing was found.

Durkel, discouraged, quit his job with Bell and said he was returning to Idaho. He was never seen again.

Bell, however, had complete faith in Durkel's tale of the train robbery and the lost gold. Bell returned to the mountains dozens of times, finding and inspecting many small lakes he encountered.

Then one day in 1971 Bell, now an old man, walked into a bar in Great Falls and proudly displayed a gold ingot! Bell found the ingot near one of the two lakes identified by Durkel years earlier. The ingot was subjected to an assay which reported it was composed of 80 percent pure gold.

Bell explained how he found the ingot. Convinced that one of the two lakes identified by Durkel years earlier held the gold, he set up camp at a location near Smith Creek and spent several days in a concentrated search of the area. Finally convinced there was nothing in the larger of the two lakes, he focused his efforts on the smaller one. For half a day and far into the night, Bell searched along the shores and in the shallow waters of the smaller lake but found nothing. Finally, as dawn was breaking over a nearby ridge, he decided to return to his camp and make some breakfast.

As Bell was winding his way back toward Smith Creek, he discovered a previously overlooked trail that approached the smaller lake from the north. The trail was obviously an old one, for decades of runoff had eroded a gully eighteen inches deep along portions of it. As Bell walked along part of the trail that passed quite close to the small lake, he was distracted by the sunlight glinting from an object just a few yards ahead. Picking it up, he discovered it was one of the gold ingots taken during the train robbery eighty-four years earlier!

Bell later opined that, in their haste to dump the gold into the lake, one of the robbers accidentally dropped one of the ingots along the trail. Encouraged by his discovery, Bell was convinced he had found the lake which contained the loot. He decided to return to Great Falls, purchase some recovery equipment, hire some help, and return to the lake to retrieve the gold.

Because Bell encountered some difficulty in procuring the recovery equipment, his return to the treasure-filled lake was delayed for several weeks. Bell was an old man at the time, and his health was in a state of deterioration. As a result of his excitement at discovering the gold and preparing for a return trip to the mountains, he suffered a severe heart attack a few weeks later and died without ever having the opportunity to return to the lake or tell anyone where it was located.

The fortune in train robbery gold still lies beneath the tranquil waters of some small, remote mountain lake west of Great Falls somewhere in the eastern slope of the Montana Rockies. Because of the heavy weight of gold, it is likely that it has sunk into the soft bottom of the lake. It is also likely that, during the century that has passed since the gold was dropped into the lake, additional silt carried into the body of water by runoff has added several inches of cover over the treasure.

Today, the value of the sacks of gold coins and the remaining ingots would be more than one million dollars.

Henry Plummer's Lost Gold

Henry Plummer is, without question, the most famous outlaw in Montana history. The western part of the state is steeped in the legend and lore of this infamous criminal, and tales of his buried fortunes have lured hundreds of treasure seekers from all across the country in search of them.

As notorious as Plummer was, very little is known about his background. It is believed he came from somewhere in the East, was highly educated, and often comported himself like a cultured gentleman. Plummer, however, discovered early in his years out West that fortunes could more easily be acquired through murder and robbery than by honest work, and since then his life had been peppered with such foul and unlawful acts.

Henry Plummer—outlaw, gambler, even lawman—was called the "Scourge of the Rockies," and if history is correct, this bandit stole more money and gold than any other famous Western outlaw.

Early in Plummer's adventurous life of crime he was chased out of Nevada by law enforcement authorities. Finding it easier to rob gold miners in California, he plied his trade there for nearly a year until local lawmen started pursuing him. From the Golden State he fled north to Washington, where he found luck as a gambler.

Even though Plummer was filling his pockets with winnings at the gambling tables in Walla Walla, he missed the adventure and excitement of robbing miners, stagecoaches, and travelers. It has been suggested by many that Plummer actually took perverse joy in being pursued by lawmen. As he was contemplating returning to a life of crime, the decision was made for him when he was chased out of Walla Walla as the result of some women trouble. He eventually drifted to Lewiston, Idaho.

At Lewiston, Plummer put together a ruthless gang of thieves and murderers, and again took up robbery and killing. After having amassed a huge fortune in gold ingots, nuggets, and coins taken from hapless miners and freight companies, the Plummer gang was constantly dogged by posses.

One of the members of the gang was a heartless killer named Jack Cleveland. In a fit of drunken rage, Cleveland once murdered a fellow gang member during an argument over some petty matter. It was rumored that even Plummer feared Cleveland and suspected the man would eventually bring trouble.

The Plummer gang often had difficulty escaping from pursuers, for Plummer himself insisted on transporting his stolen gold by mule when he traveled, instead of caching it someplace. By this time, the mule train had grown to four animals, and because their flight from the law was occasionally slowed by the sometimes reluctant pack train, the outlaws were often overtaken by pursuers, and shootouts ensued. The gang members constantly complained to their leader about the pack animals, but Plummer turned a deaf ear to them.

Because the outlaws found themselves well known to most of the law enforcement authorities in Idaho, they were constantly on the run. As successful robberies were becoming more and more difficult, Plummer decided to travel to Montana where no one knew them.

The Plummer gang arrived in the small Montana settlement of Sun River during the autumn of 1862. The outlaws immediately liked the area and believed it to be a suitable location for establishing a base of operations. Once the gang was settled into an old, abandoned ranch house Plummer located, he unloaded the gold from the mules and counted out amounts he intended to pay the members of the gang. Several of the outlaws were upset, for they had been under the impression that the gold was to be split evenly among them. Should that have been the case, they would all have become incredibly wealthy. Plummer, however, insisted the gold was really his and the men were only working for him.

The loudest disagreement came from Cleveland, who boasted that he stole as much as half of the gold Plummer claimed was his. For the time being the men settled for payment instead of equal division, but all were upset. Cleveland was furious, but remained a member of the gang.

Several weeks later, Plummer told his gang he wanted to travel alone to the gold fields near Bannock, Idaho, to determine if the area would be suitable for conducting robberies. As he was loading the gold onto the mules, several of the gang members approached him and said they didn't like the idea of him leaving with all the gold by himself. As a compromise, Plummer agreed to allow Cleveland to travel with him.

All during the trip, however, Plummer was afraid Cleveland planned to kill him and take the gold. As a result, Plummer got no sleep and was nervous and irritable the entire time they were in Bannock. The men eventually returned to Sun River having accomplished nothing.

Plummer and Cleveland came home to an empty ranch house, for the other gang members were gone to spend a few days in the saloons and gambling houses of Great Falls, about twenty miles to the east.

After unloading the gold from the mules, Plummer located a bottle of whiskey in the house and poured a drink for himself and Cleveland. While he only pretended to consume the liquor, Plummer made certain Cleveland's glass was constantly refilled. Eventually Cleveland became drunk and passed out. While he was sleeping off the effects of the alcohol, Plummer carried the accumulated gold to a location near a small creek about two hundred yards from the ranch house and buried it.

In the morning, Plummer told Cleveland he was returning to Bannock to reevaluate the possibilities of conducting some raids. Cleveland said he was going along, but when Plummer appeared all ready to travel without the gold-laden pack train, Cleveland asked him where it was. When Plummer told the outlaw he had hidden it, the enraged Cleveland pulled a gun and threatened to kill him. Plummer pulled his own gun, and in the ensuing fight, shot and killed Cleveland.

Plummer returned to Bannock and discovered numerous opportunities to make a fortune by stealing. Using his charm, he somehow was elected sheriff of the small town in May, 1863. Shortly after taking office, Plummer returned to Sun River, married a woman named Electa Bryan, and brought her back with him. In later years, Plummer's widow related that her husband had told her about the fortune in buried gold near the ranch house at Sun River, but he had never returned to retrieve it.

As sheriff of Bannock, Plummer deputized several of his old gang members and used his position to steal gold from miners and freighting companies. As was his custom, he loaded the stolen gold onto his mules and transported it to selected locations where he buried it. Anyone who rose up against him was summarily killed. During the first six-month period that Plummer was sheriff of Bannock, he and his men were responsible for the killings of 102 men!

Finally, the citizens and businessmen of Bannock decided they had had enough of the crooked lawman and organized a vigilante committee to rid the region of Plummer and his gang. One by one the vigilantes captured and hung several of Plummer's deputies. Others, fearing for their lives, fled from the area, never to return.

The vigilantes finally caught up with Plummer on January 10, 1864, and hanged him.

There were many who believed that the vigilantes had essentially organized to steal the great fortune they knew Plummer had hidden at various locations throughout the area. The vigilantes, they said, were actually little better than the Plummer gang.

Several eyewitnesses claimed that, before hanging him, the vigilantes forced Plummer to reveal the location of at least one of his gold caches. Within days after the execution, the members of the vigilante committee suddenly became wealthy.

In addition to the treasure he buried at Sun River, Plummer is known to have cached nearly two hundred thousand dollars near Birdtail Rock on the Mullan Road at the time he returned to Sun River to marry Electa. It has never been recovered.

After the marriage, Plummer took a few men and rode to Deer Lodge, about ninety miles southwest of Sun River. Here he held up a stagecoach, robbed several miners and travelers, and accumulated fifty thousand dollars' worth of gold which he buried along Cottonwood Creek. Shortly afterwards, Plummer returned to Sun River and never retrieved this cache.

Near Cascade, a few miles south of Sun River, Plummer reportedly buried three hundred thousand dollars in gold somewhere near the old St. Peter's Mission. The outlaw was hanged before he could return to this location.

Throughout the years following Plummer's death, many believed the stories about his buried gold were pure bunk, but history has proven them wrong.

In 1869, Plummer's widow returned to Sun River with a map which reputedly showed the location of the gold her former husband had buried near the ranch house. She failed to locate the treasure, but many believed she interpreted the map incorrectly and searched in the wrong place.

Henry Ford, a stepson of one of Plummer's gang members, was twelve years old in 1876 when he was playing along a shallow creek that ran near the old ranch house. Digging into the bank of the creek, young Ford unearthed several leather sacks filled with small ingots. He dragged one of the sacks home and showed his stepfather, who estimated the value of the ingots to be around sixty thousand dollars. When Ford and the stepfather returned to retrieve the rest of the gold, the youngster became disoriented and could not relocate the exact site.

In 1890, a man named Jack Young arrived at Sun River. Young's mother was a sister of a former member of the gang, and she claimed to possess a map that showed where Plummer's Sun River treasure was buried. Using the map, Young arrived at the same location near the creek where Henry Ford had discovered the ingots fourteen years earlier. Digging only a few inches into the soft earth, Young uncovered three leather saddlebags filled with gold ingots.

These are the only recorded instances of Plummer's loot being recovered. It is estimated that the notorious outlaw buried at least a million dollars' worth of gold and currency in over a dozen locations throughout western Montana, loot that has never been found.

Outlaw Skinner's Buried Gold

Following the hanging of notorious outlaw Henry Plummer in Bannock, the members of his gang who had not already been captured and lynched by vigilantes were understandably desperate to get away from the region as quickly as possible. One such gang member was Cy Skinner, who fled Bannock with around two hundred thousand dollars in gold dust, nuggets, and coins, and buried the entire hoard on a small island in the middle of the Missoula River near the town of the same name. The gold, worth over two million dollars today, is still there.

Cy Skinner knew his days were numbered on January 10, 1864, when he learned of Henry Plummer's fate. Skinner was, in fact, one of the few members of the Plummer gang who had not yet been located and captured by the wide-ranging vigilantes, and he feared his time was running out.

Within minutes of hearing of the death of Plummer, Skinner stuffed gold dust, nuggets, and coins—his share from numerous holdups and robberies—into ore sacks and saddlebags. In addition to his own gold, Skinner also packed tens of thousands of dollars' worth of loot that had belonged to other gang members, now all dead. Loading the gold onto two mules, the nervous outlaw fled from Bannack in the dark of night. Joined by six other gang members who were also fleeing the region, Skinner traveled to the settlement of Hell's Gate (now Missoula) near the eastern border of Montana.

Once at Hell's Gate, Skinner sought out his old friend Bill Hamilton. Hamilton had a small cabin on the edge of town, was known to members of the Plummer gang, and could be depended on to provide sanctuary to those fleeing from the law. Skinner moved in with Hamilton sometime in the third week of January, 1864.

Skinner knew that it would be only a matter of time before law enforcement officers learned he was in Hell's Gate, so he made tentative plans to travel north into Canada. Deciding that his two loads of gold would slow his escape, the outlaw decided to cache them someplace near Hell's Gate and return for them later. Riding up and down the banks of the Missoula River, Skinner examined the many small islands visible in the middle of the current. Selecting one he believed was suitable, Skinner recruited two gang members, Robert English and Louis Crossette, to help him bury the gold.

After loading the gold onto the mules, the three men crossed a portion of Clark's Fork and arrived at one of the small islands during the middle of the cold January night. Stuffing the dust and nuggets into three large cast-iron kettles and the coins into a brass water bucket, they dug a hole near the center of the island, placed the loot into it, covered it, and returned to Hamilton's cabin.

A few days after burying the gold, Skinner and the remaining members of the gang learned that the law had discovered they were hiding in Hell's Gate and that preparations were underway to arrest them. Crossette, who was part Blackfoot Indian, packed his few belongings and went to live with his tribe. Years later, Crossette often spoke of returning to the island in the middle of the Missoula River and retrieving Skinner's gold, but before he could do so he was stabbed to death during a saloon fight.

Robert English fled to California where he returned to his old occupation of robbing stagecoaches. After several brushes with the law, English finally retired from outlawry about ten years later.

Skinner mistakenly believed he would be safe hiding out at Hamilton's cabin until the spring thaw. On the afternoon of January 26, however, vigilantes rode up to the cabin, dragged Skinner out to a nearby creek, and hung him from the limb of a cottonwood tree. Knowing that Skinner fled Bannock with a fortune in gold, the vigilantes searched Hamilton's cabin and adjacent property for it, but found nothing. With the hanging of Skinner, the only man left alive who knew about the gold buried on the island was English.

Many years later, when residents of western Montana had long since forgotten about Henry Plummer's lesser-known gang members, Robert English, who by this time had changed his name to Charley Duchase, returned to Hell's Gate. English spent several days riding along the river searching for the island on which he, Skinner, and Crossette had buried the gold, but was unable to determine which was the correct one. The former outlaw observed that the river had altered its course somewhat and everything looked different. He also stated that there appeared to be more islands than he remembered from 1864. In fact, at the time when English was inspecting the river the streamflow was very low, exposing more islands than normally encountered. Confused and unsure, English eventually abandoned his search for the buried treasure and returned to California.

In 1894, a man arrived in Missoula from St. Paul, Minnesota, to search for Skinner's gold. He possessed an old map which he claimed showed the location of the buried treasure on one of the islands in the Missoula River. For several weeks the man rowed out to the various islands and excavated numerous holes, but found nothing.

Ed Taichert, a longtime Missoula resident, learned of Skinner's gold cache in the 1930s. For years, Taichert collected and studied every fragment of information he could find concerning the tale. Finally, Taichert decided he was certain he knew which island contained the buried gold.

Selecting the third island downstream from the bridge which leads to Montana State University, Taichert waited until the streamflow was lower than normal. One night he gathered up pick and shovel, waded the river, and proceeded to dig several holes at one end of the island. While excavating the third hole, Taichert's shovel struck a metal bucket about six inches below the surface. Excited, Taichert removed the bucket and refilled the hole. Returning home, he examined the contents of the bucket and was delighted to discover it contained several thousand dollars' worth of gold coins! Taichert was convinced he had located the Skinner cache and made plans to return to the island the next evening and retrieve the rest of it.

That evening, however, heavy rains caused the river to rise. The next morning when Taichert appeared at the river bank, he discovered the river was near flood stage and all of the islands were underwater. The river remained high and swift for nearly two weeks, delaying Taichert's search. Finally, the water level subsided and he was able to return to the island, only to discover its configuration had been altered as a result of the raging flood waters. For several days he examined the island, dug holes, and poked around, but he could not relocate the exact site from which he had earlier removed the iron bucket.

Weeks passed and Taichert received an opportunity to invest in a mining enterprise at Lincoln, about sixty miles east of Missoula. After disposing of the coins he had discovered, Taichert purchased an interest in the mine, bought some equipment, and left Missoula.

In 1957, Taichert retired and returned to Missoula. For the next six years he rowed out to the third island from the bridge and searched for Skinner's gold at every opportunity. Finally, in 1963 when he was eighty years old, he abandoned the search.

Taichert, as do many others, believed the greatest portion of Skinner's gold remains buried on the island. Because the rising and lowering river alternately erodes material from one end of the island and deposits it on the other, constantly changing its size and shape, Taichert believed that maps purporting to show the location of the treasure are useless.

Skinner's gold, worth well over two million dollars today, is still concealed beneath a foot or so of sand and gravel on a small island in the middle of the Missoula River.

Springer's Lost Lode

Old man Springer arrived in the small but bustling mining camp of Deer Lodge in the spring of 1868. Springer was older than most of the prospectors and miners in the area, but no less energetic and enthusiastic about discovering gold and becoming wealthy.

Thomas O. Springer came from Sycamore, Illinois, by way of the California gold fields. Try as he did, Springer had no luck in California, so he drifted to Montana. Along the way he picked up a great deal of knowledge about mining and gold.

Preferring to work alone, Springer packed into the mountains east of Deer Lodge for long periods of time. He panned the numerous small streams that trickled through the canyons and searched the igneous, intrusive rock outcrops for signs of goldbearing quartz. Every six weeks or so he would return to Deer Lodge to purchase supplies. It was clear that Springer had little or no money, for he would occasionally work off the cost of his purchases by performing chores for the storekeepers.

Springer's life changed during the summer of 1870. Coming in from the mountains following one of his usual trips, the prospector purchased his supplies with nuggets of pure gold.

When questioned, Springer was vague about his new find. He did mention, however, that he had located a rich, exposed vein of goldbearing quartz. The gold was so plentiful in the seam, he said, that he could pry it out with a knife.

Having discovered gold in large quantities should have put an end to Springer's problems, but it only created others. Once word of his discovery got around town, men began to follow him on his return trips into the mountains. Springer once said he spent more time evading trackers than he did actually extracting gold from his find. Because he wanted the location of his mine kept secret, Springer refused to file a claim on the site, fearing that the posted location would bring unwanted visitors into the vicinity. Springer gradually grew paranoid about protecting his discovery and came to town less often. When he did arrive in Deer Lodge, he remained only long enough to make a few purchases and then departed, usually in the dark of night.

Springer continued to mine gold from the rich vein over the next two years. Though he spent some of his wealth in Deer Lodge for supplies and equipment, he hid the greater portion of it. During one of his trips to town he purchased two dozen canvas ore sacks and told the proprietor he was filling them with nuggets of pure gold from his diggings and hiding them in a place near the mine where no one could ever find them. Springer also claimed the mine was camouflaged so well that no one would ever detect its location, even if they were standing within twenty feet of it.

As time wore on, Springer, already in his sixties, found the physical exertion of packing into and out of the mountains hard on his tired old body. His health was failing and he found he had to stop often to catch his breath while walking to his secret location. On at least two occasions he believed he suffered minor heart attacks.

One afternoon in August of 1872, Springer, in an uncharacteristic move, appeared in Deer Lodge to recruit partners to join him in his mining operation. He explained he was getting too old and feeble to continue traveling to the site and digging the gold from the quartz vein by himself. After visiting with several prospective partners, he selected three men—John Hildreth, Sam Scott, and John Stearns. The three were well known and respected around Deer Lodge as honest, competent miners.

The next morning, Springer and his new partners rode out of Deer Lodge into the mountains. They were leading a string of pack mules loaded with mining equipment and enough provisions to last for a month. The three newcomers, eager to view the goldbearing vein so often rumored about during the past two years, were beside themselves with excitement.

After traveling about fifteen difficult miles through a series of winding, boulder-choked canyons east of Deer Lodge, Springer called for a halt to rest both men and animals. Breathing heavily, he sat down on a rock clutching his chest. After a while, Springer told the men to proceed up the canyon about another mile and set up camp near a small spring located there. He said he would go in search of a deer and try to bring back some venison for supper. The miner told the men that come morning it would only be another couple of miles to the mine.

As the three partners rode away leading the pack mules, they waved farewell to Springer, who had picked up his rifle and walked into the nearby forest. It was the last time anyone would see him alive.

Evening came, and a deep chill descended on the narrow canyon. With the horses and mules hobbled, a campfire burning, and bedrolls laid out on the ground, the three men waited for Springer. All night long they remained awake, expecting the old-timer to arrive at any moment, but he never appeared. As soon as it was light Hildreath, Scott, and Stearns saddled their horses and rode back down the trail in search of Springer. They looked for the old man until well past noon, but found no trace of him. They decided to ride into Deer Lodge and get help.

The next morning a search party consisting of about twenty men returned to the canyon where Springer was last seen. Around noon, the old prospector was finally found seated against a thick pine in a dense clump of trees, dead from a massive heart attack. In death, Springer took with him the secret to the location of the rich goldbearing quartz and what must have been a very large cache of gold he had extracted from the vein.

Knowing they were in the vicinity of Springer's secret mine, the three partners spent the next several weeks combing the area in search of it. So remote was its location and so well hidden was the mine that they were never able to find anything. Eventually they gave up and returned to Deer Lodge.

Over the years others have ridden and walked into the rugged mountains east of Deer Lodge in search of Springer's lost lode and cache, but the gold has eluded them all.

NEVADA

1. The Lost Hardin Silver
2. The Curse of the Lost Sheepherder's Mine
3. Lost Blue Bucket Placer Gold
4. Buried Wells-Fargo Gold

The Lost Hardin Silver

Allen Hardin and two good friends were traveling west in an immigrant wagon train when they accidentally stumbled onto what many consider to be the richest deposit of silver in North America. Unable to carry away but a small amount of the precious ore in their already overloaded wagons, the men proceeded on to California.

Despite a decade of searching, Hardin never relocated the immense deposit, and for more than a hundred years others have roamed the remote and forbidding Black Rock Range of northwestern Nevada, looking for the fortune in almost pure silver ore believed to exist there.

The year was 1849. Hardin, his companions, and dozens of others were members of a wagon train bound for California from St. Louis, Missouri. The prospect of the rich gold fields, abundant farmlands, and commercial opportunities in the Golden State appealed to the three men, so they pooled their money, purchased a wagon and team, and headed west to meet new challenges and hopefully grow successful and wealthy.

After weeks of rough and difficult travel, the wagon train arrived at a point near the base of Pahute Peak, the southernmost promontory associated with the Black Rock Range. The wagon train pulled up into a meadow between the peak and Mud Meadows River just to the west. Here the leader of the train decided to spend a few days resting animals and travelers alike, and to allow the stock to graze on the rich grasses found in the meadow.

Tired of the usual meals of biscuits and dried meat eaten along the trail, Hardin and his friends decided to ride into the Black Rock Range one morning and hunt game. For several hours they rode and hiked in the rugged foothills but encountered no game at all save some birds, which were so far away that no one was able to get off a shot. Dejected, the three men decided to return to the camp around mid-afternoon.

On the way back, they traveled along a rough, seldom-used trail that paralleled a freshly eroded gully on their left. From the appearance of the gully, it was clear that the five-foot-deep cut was the result of recent torrential rains and turbulent runoff cutting through the highly weathered and weakened rock found in this part of the range.

As the three rode along, Hardin glanced into the gully and saw several fist-sized chunks of milk-colored, metallic-looking rock. Calling for a halt, Hardin dismounted and, along with the others, slid into the gully to investigate.

At the bottom of the eroded cut, the men found dozens of pieces of the white metal lying about. Inspecting the sides of the gully, Hardin noticed that several other larger pieces were protruding from the sides. On the far side of the gully, one of Hardin's companions found a thick vein of the strange-looking metal.

Picking up several pieces from the floor of the cut, the men found them to be heavy for their size. Hardin poked and pried at one of the chunks with the point of his knife and discovered it to be soft and malleable. Slicing off a thin section, he found he could roll and compress it between his fingers. Hardin pronounced the metal to be lead.

The men were happy at having discovered what they believed was lead, for the metal was used to fashion bullets and was relatively scarce among the members of the wagon train. As they gathered up several pieces with the intention of placing it in their saddlebags, one of the men made an astounding discovery. Closely inspecting the outcrop found in the wall of the gully, he determined the metal was not lead at all, but almost pure silver.

Noting the size and thickness of the vein as well as the numerous scattered pieces on the floor of the gully, Hardin realized they had just discovered an incredible fortune in silver ore!

Their hearts thumped in anticipation of the great wealth they believed would soon be theirs, as the three men loaded about twenty-five pounds of the metal into their saddlebags and returned to the encampment.

On arriving, they announced their discovery and enlisted the aid of several fellow immigrants to return to the gully with them to bring out more of the silver. Unfortunately, most of the trail-weary travelers were unimpressed with the find. For one thing, many did not believe it was silver at all. For another, the tired travelers were anxious to get back on the trail to California now that the stock had been rested and watered.

Hardin and his companions initially considered remaining in the area and mining the silver, but as the threat of hostile Paiute Indians in the region was very real, they opted to make the journey with the others. Taking note of specific landmarks such as Pahute Peak and the Mud Meadows River, the three men vowed to return to the area to extract the silver immediately after reaching civilization in California.

Several days later, in the town of Shasta in northern California, Hardin showed some samples of the ore to local miners, who pronounced it the purest silver they had ever seen. But when Hardin invited them to return to the Black Rock Range with him to help mine the silver they declined, saying they were more interested in searching for gold.

Out of funds and in need of work, Hardin and his friends were unable to return immmediately to the Black Rock Range. The three men took jobs around Shasta and saved their money in anticipation of the long journey back to the remote gully filled with pure silver ore.

Months passed, and the three men had not put back enough money to finance a return trip to the Black Rock Range. The dream of riches in faraway Nevada grew dim. The three friends drifted apart after several months and eventually lost touch with one another.

Sometime during the spring of 1850, Hardin shipped a sample of the silver he took from the gully to a professional assayer in San Francisco. The assayer, in a return missive, stated it was very high quality ore. Encouraged by this report, Hardin continued to remain enthusiastic about returning to the Black Rock Range, but for the moment he was preoccupied with earning a living.

Hardin eventually settled in Petaluma, California, north of San Francisco. He took up farming and made a decent living but never lost his desire to return to the Nevada mountains for his silver. In Petaluma, Harding met a man named Frederick Alberding. The two became friends, and in time Hardin related the tale of his discovery of the silver. Alberding, who had considerable prospecting and mining experience in Nevada, said that he had heard the same story from a man several months earlier. It turned out the source of the story was one of Hardin's original traveling companions.

Alberding proposed that the two of them put together an expedition and return to the Black Rock Range to relocate the silver. Hardin agreed, and eventually seven other men were enlisted to accompany them and participate in the search and profits.

Nine years after discovering the silver in the rugged foothills of the Black Rock Range, Hardin and his party arrived at the site near Mud Meadows River where the wagon train had stopped to camp. The next morning, leaving two men to look after the wagons and stock, Hardin and the others struck out in search of the silver-laden gully.

As they rode through the rough and barren landscape, Hardin soon realized he was lost. He did not recognize any landmarks, nothing looked familiar, and he had difficulty with directions and orientation.

For two years the men searched. Others would occasionally join the party, and sometimes there were as many as fifty men combing the hills for the silver.

One of the original members of Hardin's party, M.S. Thompson, agreed that, based on Harding's description of the gully, it had been suddenly and violently carved into the weathered and crumpled bedrock as the result of intense runoff after a torrential downpour. Subsequent rainfall during the intervening years could just as likely cover the gully with debris and sediment washing down from the higher elevations.

During the late spring of 1860, word reached the men that the Paiute Indians were rising up and had recently defeated a large calvalry unit not far from the search area. Fearing for their lives, the men abandoned the region and returned to California. When the Indians were finally defeated and captured several months later, none of the original members of the expedition returned to the Black Rock Range. It is unknown what became of Hardin.

During the years that followed, however, hundreds of prospectors, adventurers, and treasure hunters who had heard the tale of the mysterious gully entered the Black Rock Range in search of Hardin's lost silver. Most returned discouraged and broke, but a few actually located silver elsewhere in the range and opened up small mines.

Geologists explain that the formation of new gullies in weak and fractured rock is not an uncommon event during severe rainstorms and associated runoff. They state that it is also common for such excavations to be covered up by subsequent runoff traveling at slower velocities and carrying large amounts of sediment. Perhaps some lucky searcher will arrive in a remote canyon in the foothills of the Black Rock Range following a severe storm and rediscover Hardin's elusive gully filled with a fortune in silver ore.

The Curse of the Lost Sheepherder's Mine

Somewhere in the Jarbridge Mountains in northeastern Nevada near the Idaho border lies a rich yet strangely elusive gold deposit. This gold has been found several times—in fact, some of it has even been mined—yet each time, whoever has come in contact with the gold has died.

It is believed that the gold in these mountains was initially discovered by two Mormons sometime during the late 1870s. The men were members of a party which set out from Salt Lake City in search of promising land on which to begin farming. The party spent several weeks exploring parts of northeastern Nevada but found little that appealed to them—water was scarce and hostile Indians were plentiful. While camped near the small settlement of Jarbridge, two members of the party decided to ride into the nearby mountains to explore. What they found was a considerable quantity of gold in one of the canyons. When the two reported their find to the leader of the group, they were informed that mining for gold was not an acceptable profession for a devout Mormon. The two men said nothing more, but after the group returned to Salt Lake City several weeks later, they acquired provisions and retraced the route back to the Jarbridge Mountains.

They easily relocated the canyon and found a rich vein of gold near its origin high in the mountains. Slowly and laboriously they proceeded to dig the ore from the canyon wall, eventually excavating a narrow shaft.

In their spare time, the two men built a small, crude log cabin in which they slept, ate, and stored their accumulated gold. In addition to taking gold from the vein, they worked long hours panning and picking it from placer deposits found in the stream on the canyon floor.

Two or three times a year, the Mormons would carry their gold to Elko, some eighty miles to the south, and exchange it for supplies and cash. The purity and abundance of the gold sparked the interest of several Elko residents, but the two miners remained vague about the location of their diggings. On several occasions they were followed back into the mountains, but each time they eluded their trackers.

One winter, probably during the second or third year the Mormons were working their mine, snowfall in the mountains was heavier than usual, piling up several feet deep on the steep flanks. In the region where the miners had their cabin, a tremendous avalanche occurred during January that destroyed everything in its path for hundreds of yards down the slope. Those who entered the region following the event claimed that it had completely obliterated the cabin, and the miners were never seen again. Several people searched for the location of the rich gold mine, but it was was never found. Most believed it was covered by rock and debris during the avalanche.

In 1885, stagecoaches regularly stopped in the small town of Jarbridge. Here, fresh horses were supplied and drivers and passengers alike enjoyed a hot meal and spent a quiet evening until the next morning when it was time to depart.

Arriving early one afternoon, a stagecoach driver decided to borrow a horse and ride into the nearby mountains to look around. As he rode into one particular canyon, the driver noticed some color along the stream bed. Upon investigation, it turned out to be several impressive gold nuggets! Following the stream on up the canyon, he came across evidence of what appeared to be a mine, but the entrance was blocked with rock and soil.

When the driver returned to the stage station, he gave a piece of the gold to the station operator and asked him to mail it off and have it assayed. Several weeks later, the assay report had arrived and was waiting for the driver—it declared the ore to be extremely rich. Knowing that the gold was abundant in the stream bed and quite likely in the mine, the driver resigned his position, purchased some mining supplies, and disappeared into the mountains. At about the same time, the Paiute Indians were roaming the countryside throughout northern Nevada, attacking immigrants and raiding ranches and small communities. Shortly after the stagecoach driver ventured into the Jarbridge Mountains, the Paiutes were observed entering the same region. The driver was never seen again and it is believed he was killed by the Indians.

By now the residents of Jarbridge and the surrounding area believed that the gold in the mountains brought nothing but bad luck to anyone who attemptd to retrieve it. They often spoke of a curse on the area, one likely placed there by the Indians, who resented the intrusion of whites into the region.

In 1891, a prospector named Ross arrived in Jarbridge and inquired about the likelihood of locating gold in the mountains.

The story of the cursed gold was related, but rather than being discouraged the miner perceived it as a challenge. He set out the next day in search of the ore.

Within a few days, Ross discovered the canyon which contained the gold-rich stream. Encouraged by the size and quantity of the nuggets he found, the prospector followed the narrow stream up the steep canyon and found an extremely rich vein of gold. It is not known if he located the mine that had been excavated by the two Mormons.

Running low on provisions, Ross decided to return to Jarbridge. He marked the location of the vein by placing his pick and shovel upright in the ground a short distance from it, near the head of the canyon. Several hours later on his way to the settlement, Ross came upon a remote sheep camp located on the east bank of the Jarbridge River. Thinking he might find a cup of coffee and some conversation, Ross approached the sheepherder and introduced himself. The sheepherder, a man named Ishman, enjoyed Ross's company and invited him to spend the night before going on to town. The herder worked for John Pence, a successful rancher who lived near the town.

That evening, while sitting around the campfire sipping coffee, Ross revealed his amazing discovery to the sheepherder, describing the canyon, the stream, and the place where he left his pick and shovel. Ross told Ishman that if anything ever happened to him, Ishman was welcome to the gold.

The next morning Ross departed for Jarbridge, where he purchased supplies with several gold nuggets he had gathered from the floor of the canyon. Hefting his load, he left town and vanished into the mountains. Ross, like the Mormons and the stagecoach driver before him, was never seen again.

The following spring, after the heavy snows had melted from the higher elevations, herder Ishman became curious as to how his friend Ross was succeeding with his gold-mining activities high in the remote canyon. When he found an opportunity, he used the directions provided months earlier by Ross and hiked the long distance from the camp to the gold-filled canyon.

Following a punishing climb of several hours in the high altitudes, the sheepherder arrived at a point where he discovered Ross's pick and shovel stuck in the ground, just as it had been described. But next to the tools, Ishman found something that caused gooseflesh to rise along his spine—the bleached bones of a human skeleton!

Although there was no way the skeleton could be positively identified as that of Ross, the sheepherder was certain that it was.

On his return trip down the canyon, Ishman picked up several gold nuggets and stuffed them in his pockets. Back at the sheep camp, he examined the nuggets and grew fascinated with the prospect of becoming rich. Afterwards, at every opportunity, Ishman would hike into the canyon and collect placer gold from the stream.

As the sheepherder prospected and panned his way along the little stream during the ensuing months, he kept an eye out for the vein of gold he believed must exist nearby, which supplied the rich float that he found in the canyon. Eventually he encountered the old Mormon mine, removed the covering of debris that blocked the entrance, and discovered the thick, rich seam of gold within.

For reasons unknown to anyone but himself, Ishman decided to tell his employer about his discovery. Collecting a sackful of gold ore, along with the skull he believed to be Ross's, the sheepherder went to John Pence and explained all that had transpired since he had met the miner a year earlier.

On examining the samples of gold, Pence realized the incredible fortune that must lie high in the Jarbridge Mountains. Pence wanted to go to the canyon immediately, but as winter was coming on and the snows were starting to fall in the high country, travel was impossible. Ishman agreed to take Pence to the mine in the spring, as soon as the snow melted from the higher altitudes.

When spring finally arrived and patches of bare ground could be seen on the high slopes, Pence and Ishman rode into the mountains. Soon the two reached a point where it became too dangerous to travel on horseback so, tying the animals to a bush, they proceeded on foot.

Up the steep mountain the two men hiked, Pence often calling for a halt so he could catch his breath. Higher and higher into the rarified air they climbed, and when it seemed like the exhausted Pence could go no farther, Ishman informed him that the gold-filled canyon was only about a quarter of a mile away.

Ishman proceeded another half dozen steps when he suddenly stiffened, grabbed his head with both hands, and crumpled to the ground, unconscious.

Pence, nearly done in himself, managed with great difficulty to drag Ishman back to the horses, tie him on to his mount, and return to Jarbridge. The next day the rancher loaded the still unconscious man into a wagon and transported him to the nearest doctor, more than one hundred miles away.

Ishman remained in a coma for several days. His ensuing death, according to the doctor, was the result of a severe cerebral hemorrhage.

With Ishman, death claimed the last man who knew the location of the gold-laden canyon and the rich vein of ore somewhere deep in the Jarbridge Mountains. Since Ishman's demise, the elusive site has been referred to as the Lost Sheepherder's Mine. His passing served to revive the tales of the old Indian curse on the gold, which many still believe was responsible for the deaths of the sheepherder and the others.

Will someone eventually locate the Lost Sheepherder's Mine and claim the huge fortune which is apparently there for the taking? Or will they, like the others, fall victim to the curse?

Lost Blue Bucket Placer Gold

Of all the tales of lost gold and buried treasures associated with Nevada, none is recounted more frequently than that of the Lost Blue Bucket Placer. According to the story, a fantastic fortune in placer gold was accidentally discovered by a group of Oregon-bound immigrants while traveling through a small canyon near the Nevada-Oregon border. Several nuggets were collected, but no one recognized them for what they were at the time. When it was discovered later that the nuggets were gold, several immigrants returned to the area in an unsuccessful attempt to relocate the canyon. Today, the site of the Lost Blue Bucket Placer remains one of the biggest mysteries in Nevada.

In 1845, a large wagon train slowly made its way along the Humboldt Trail across the extremely rugged and unpopulated terrain of northern Nevada. The train was composed of more than a hundred heavily laden wagons pulled by oxen. Most of the members of the train were bound for the rich farming country of southern Oregon, while others would travel to California. Those continuing on to Oregon parted company with the California-bound immigrants near the present-day town of Imlay, and proceeded along the Applegate-Lassen trail through what is now Humboldt County and on into Oregon.

The Applegate-Lassen Trail was more difficult than anything the immigrants had experienced thus far. Much of it had been washed away as a result of recent torrential rains, and a great deal of time was lost searching for routes around and across the deep gullies created by rapid runoff. In some places, the wagons and stock had to be lowered down steep inclines using ropes and the efforts of dozens of men.

This part of the trip passed through Paiute country, and the immigrants had to be constantly on the lookout for the hostile Indians, who resented the intrusion of whites into their homelands. The trail was dotted with the graves of less fortunate travelers who had encountered the warring Paiutes.

One morning, following a particularly difficult procession up a steep section of trail, the wagon train proceeded through a shallow canyon not far from the Nevada-Oregon border. The immigrants knew they were only a few days away from their destination and their spirits were high. Anticipating the end of their long and arduous journey, they sang as they guided the wagons along the rocky bottom of the canyon.

The wagons rolled along, jouncing over rocks and clattering on the bare granite floor of the canyon. The many youngsters in the party ran alongside, playing in the narrow stream that paralleled the trail. Now and again the bright gleam of small, shiny stones would catch the eyes of the children and they would pick them up. One child challenged another that she could find more of the shiny rocks than any of the others, and a playful contest soon evolved. As the children excitedly gathered the gleaming yellow stones, they threw them into the wooden utility buckets that were tied to the sides of many of the wagons. The buckets, purchased from a St. Louis manufacturer, were all painted blue and were used to haul water and various items.

The men, their attention directed toward keeping the wagons on the trail and remaining constantly on the lookout for Indians, ignored the playful antics of the children and paid no attention to the growing collections of small yellowish stones in the bottoms of several of the empty blue buckets.

Several days later, when the wagon train arrived at its destination, the business of unpacking and setting up temporary shelters and housekeeping got underway. As the blue buckets were needed to carry items and transport water, those carrying the shiny stones were emptied and put into use. Some of the children managed to gather up their shiny stones before they were discarded, however, and kept them among their few personal belongings.

A few months later, a party of miners stopped at the new immigrant settlement. They had recently come from a successful gold mining-venture in the mountains of northern California and were on their way back East to set themselves up in business with their new-found wealth. While visiting with some of the immigrants around a campfire one evening, one of the miners observed a child playing with several small, glistening stones. The light of the campfire reflecting off of the yellow stones caught the visitor's attention. Asking the child if he could see one of them, the miner examined the nugget closely. Presently he asked where it had come from, and the father of the child explained that the children had picked them up from the bottom of a small canyon many miles to the southeast in Nevada.

The miner, holding the nugget out to the man, informed him it was the purest gold he had ever seen!The remaining nuggets were inspected and they, like the first, were found to be gold.

Several of the settlers, excited about the prospect of a great fortune in gold awaiting them on the floor of that shallow canyon several days' ride to the southeast, immediately began preparations to return. Within the next two days, a party of men had outfitted themselves and ridden out of the settlement to try to relocate the gold-filled canyon.

The expedition was doomed from the start. One evening, while camping in a thicket along a small stream in southeastern Oregon, most of their horses were stolen by Indians. Undeterred, however, they proceeded—some mounted, some on foot.

As they approached the area where they believed they would find the canyon, they were set upon by Indians and barely escaped with their lives. Completely frightened, they returned to the settlement and vowed never to go back to the area again.

While the enthusiasm of the settlers for locating the gold had dimmed somewhat, their penchant for relating the story did not, and many a visitor to the immigrant settlement heard the tale of the Lost Blue Bucket Placer. Several visitors who heard the story made attempts to find the canyon but turned back due to hostile Indians, scarcity of water, and sometimes just plain bad luck.

One day, a few years later, a physician visited the immigrant settlement. He, too, was told the tale of the Lost Blue Bucket Placer. When they had finished their story, however, the townsfolk were treated to an even more fascinating one by the doctor.

The physician had spent several months in Paiute country in northeastern Nevada, near the Black Rock and Granite Ranges, treating soldiers, settlers, and even Indians for various wounds and ailments. The physician had a large gold nugget attached to his watch fob and one day, while treating a Paiute Indian for an infection, he pulled out the timepiece to check the hour. On seeing the gold nugget, the Indian expressed interest. When the doctor explained what it was, the Indian told the doctor of a canyon located several days' ride to the north, where similar nuggets could be found in abundance in the little stream that trickled through the cut. The description of the canyon provided by the Indian matched those given by the settlers.

Paiutes occasionally visited old Fort Bidwell in northeastern California to obtain supplies. In many cases the Indians paid for their purchases with gold nuggets. When asked where they obtained the gold, the Indians always pointed eastward and told of a canyon where the nuggets could be easily picked up out of the shallow stream that flowed along the bottom. Several traders at the fort attempted to follow the Indians when they departed, but the Paiutes eluded them.

The Lost Blue Bucket Placer has been the object of hundreds of expeditions and search parties into northeastern Nevada for more then a hundred years. Some people come out of the region with a bit of gold, but history has yet to record the rediscovery of the gold-rich canyon through which the immigrants traveled in 1845.

With the passage of time, much of the original route of the Applegate-Lassen trail has been lost. But even if the old trail should be rediscovered using documents and journals, it might not help. In the intervening years, the region in question has been subjected to earthquakes and violent flash floods, which have rearranged much of the landscape and topography from what it was 150 years ago.

That there is gold in the region has been substantiated many times. Prospectors and miners have located the precious ore in various places throughout much of northern Nevada, but the canyon containing the Lost Blue Bucket Placer has always eluded the searchers.

The search, as well as the mystery, continues.

Buried Wells-Fargo Gold

Early one morning in 1885, a Wells-Fargo stage was rumbling across the Nevada desert from Virginia City toward the U.S. mint at Carson City to the southwest. Stagecoach driver William Manners guided the team of six spirited horses along the thirteen-mile trail, as guard Mike O'Fallon whistled a tune and looked out across the desert. The two men had made this trip dozens of times without mishap and were expecting no problems on this day. They were in for a rude awakening.

Lashed to the top of the stage was a heavy metal strongbox packed with sixty-two thousand dollars' worth of gold coins and bullion. Tied next to the strongbox and in the canvas boot at the rear of the coach were several pieces of luggage belonging to the five passengers riding inside.

Just after crossing the Carson River, Manners and O'Fallon spotted Carson City about a mile ahead, the outlines of a few buildings on the outskirts of the town just barely discernable. The most prominent of the structures was the territorial prison.

With the trip almost over, the two men slowed the team a bit and discussed what they would do with their spare time in town after unloading the stage.

Suddenly, from behind the dense brush along one side of the trail, four men leaped in front of the oncoming stage. Two of them grabbed the lead horses and brought them to a halt while the others held guns on Manners and O'Fallon.

Once the horses were stopped, one of the bandits climbed onto the stage, untied the strongbox, and tossed it onto the ground. Another walked to the side of the coach and ordered the passengers out, telling them to place their valuables in a canvas sack he produced. The take from the passengers amounted to about two thousand dollars in coins and jewelry.

The robbery of the Wells-Fargo stagecoach and its passengers took only a few minutes. When it was over, the bandits ordered everyone back on board and on to Carson City. As the coach proceeded down the road, O'Fallon turned and watched two of the bandits pick up the heavy strongbox and, with great difficulty, attempt to carry it on foot out into the Nevada desert. He knew they would not get far with it that way.

On arriving at Carson City, Manners and O'Fallon immediately notified the law enforcement authorities, and within a half an hour a heavily armed posse set out in pursuit of the robbers.

With no trouble at all the posse members located the place where the stage had been stopped and robbed. Plainly visible on the sandy ground were the tracks of four men leading out into the desert.

In a matter of minutes the bandits were spotted—minus the strongbox—walking across the open ground about a mile from the road.

When the outlaws heard the hoofbeats of the approaching lawmen they turned, drew their revolvers, and fired at the oncoming riders. Dozens of shots were exchanged. None of the posse members was hit, but one of the outlaws was killed during the initial fusillade. Two more managed to escape and reach some horses they had hidden in a nearby ravine. The fourth bandit, a Mexican, was captured and taken to the jail at Carson City.

While the identities of the two escaped robbers were never officially recorded, many believed they were the same men who were killed during a similar holdup attempt near the Arizona border several weeks later.

The Mexican, Manuel Gonzales, was detained in a jail cell that evening for questioning. Despite facing a long prison term, the outlaw refused to tell the law officers the names of his accomplices or where the strongbox and the items taken from the passengers were buried.

The next day, three deputies returned to the site of the robbery and combed the area on horseback and on foot in search of the strongbox or some sign of a fresh excavation. They found neither.

What had become of the gold? Clearly the outlaws had been unable to carry the heavy, gold-filled container very far, and they had had plenty of time to bury it before fleeing into the desert. It had to be someplace close to the road—but where?

Within a few weeks, Gonzales was tried, found guilty, and sentenced to twenty years at hard labor in the Nevada Territorial Prison. It was located just a few blocks from the courthouse near the point where the Virginia City-Carson City road entered the town.

After serving eight years of his sentence, Gonzales contracted tuberculosis and had to be hospitalized. Because Gonzales could not receive the proper medical care in the prison, and because he had been a model prisoner and was regarded as harmless, the governor issued a pardon to the Mexican. Wells-Fargo officials agreed to this, as they reasoned that, once out of prison, Gonzales would return to the site where the strongbox was buried.

From the day of his release and for several months thereafter, Gonzales was watched constantly by a team of Wells-Fargo agents. To their surprise and disappointment, Gonzales never left downtown Carson City.

In poor health and unable to hold down a job, Gonzales wandered the streets of Carson City begging for handouts and food. Eventually, a local butcher named George Stark took pity on the poor wretch and gave him a job sweeping up the market at the end of the day. In addition to the meager salary he paid Gonzales, Stark allowed the ex-convict to sleep in a storeroom located behind the shop.

Aware of his role in the robbery of the Wells-Fargo stagecoach eight years earlier, Stark often tried to guide the Mexican into conversation about the event in the hope of deriving some clue as to where the gold was buried. In every case, Gonzales would smile and deftly steer the conversation on to another topic. One evening, however, while visiting with Stark, the Mexican informed his employer that he had been able to see the location where the chest was buried from his prison window!

Several years passed, and Gonzales's health grew worse. One day, realizing he would not live much longer, the Mexican called Stark to his bedside and told him he would show him where the stongbox was buried in gratitude for his kindness.

Overjoyed, Stark quickly saddled two horses and brought them around to Gonzales's room. As the butcher helped the weak and emaciated Mexican onto a horse, Gonzales let out a stifled moan, grabbed his chest, and pitched over the opposite side and onto the ground, dead from a heart attack.

Stark was frustrated at not being able to locate the gold. Several weeks later, recalling that the Mexican claimed he could see its location from his prison window, Stark requested permission to scan the countryside from that vantage point. Unfortunately, the view took in an area of several square miles.

For some years, Stark searched the region alongside the Virginia City-Carson City road for the buried strongbox, but was unsuccessful. Over time, as the story of the stolen strongbox spread throughout the area, treasure hunters came from miles around to engage in the search, but the gold remained hidden.

During the past three decades, searchers using sophisticated electronic equipment have combed the area in search of the lost gold-filled strongbox. They have been continually frustrated by the high metallic content of the rock and soil in the area.

Somewhere along the old road, a short distance beyond the historic city limits of Carson City and beneath a few inches of desert soil, lies a heavy metal strongbox filled with gold. At today's values, this elusive cache would easily be worth more than a million dollars.

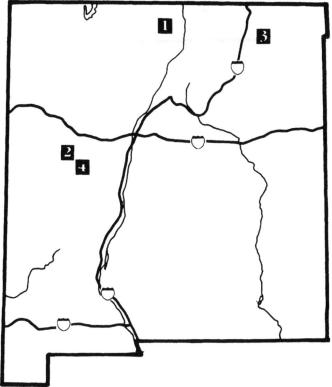

NEW MEXICO

1. A Fortune in Gold Ingots in Cancino Arroyo
2. Lost Treasure of the Lava Beds
3. Madame Barcelo's Lost $500,000 in Gold Coins
4. Lost Train Robbery Loot in Cibola County

A Fortune in Gold Ingots in Cancino Arroyo

In a remote, sandy arroyo located between the Rio Grande and the small town of Tres Piedras in northern New Mexico, dozens of gold ingots believed to be worth more than a million dollars lie buried under a few feet of sand. There are several people alive today who claim to know the exact location where the gold can be found, but the passage of time and the vagaries of the soft and porous bottom of the arroyo has rendered recovery extremely difficult.

The events leading to the ultimate deposition of the gold ingots in the arroyo are a blend of incredible circumstance, misfortune, and fate. On August 9, 1880, the notorious outlaw Porter Stockton and a companion were involved in a gunfight in Cimarron, a growing community located at the north end of the Sangre de Cristo mountain range. Two men were killed, and the outlaws immediately fled westward toward their hideout in Gallegos Canyon near Tres Piedras.

After they crossed the Rio Grande, the sky clouded over and a light rain started to fall. As the day wore on, the rain became heavier, making travel difficult. By evening the storm grew violent and the rain came in thick sheets, washing out the road in places. Unable to discern landmarks, Stockton and his companion became lost and inadvertently rode into the opening of an arroyo. A short time later, a party of three men on horseback leading two heavily laden mules were traveling eastward along the same trail. A month earlier these three men, following the directions provided on an old map, had located a long-hidden cache of Spanish gold ingots deep in an abandoned mine shaft somewhere in Arizona. Packing as many of the gold bars as they could carry into stout leather panniers, they loaded them onto the mules and were returning to their homes in Colorado when they were caught in the storm. New to this territory and uncertain about the washed-out trail, they spotted the tracks of the two fleeing outlaws and, presuming the riders were following a well-established trail, followed them into the arroyo.

As Stockton and his companion rode deeper into the channel, they noted the walls were getting higher and steeper. At the same time, the small stream that normally trickled along the bottom of the wash was growing into a surging, muddy current that was already a foot deep. Realizing they were lost and fearful there was no outlet from the arroyo, Stockton suggested they return to the opening and continue westward. The outlaws were also afraid they might be caught in a flash flood. As the two men rode back along the floor of the arroyo, occasional flashes of lightning illuminated the way.

Rounding a bend in the deep channel, Stockton and his companion were startled by the appearance of the three riders coming toward them. As the newcomers were framed in the flash of the next lightning strike, Stockton jumped to the conclusion that they were part of a posse of lawmen from Cimarron sent to track them down. With a yell, Stockton yanked his pistol from his holster and spurred his horse toward the three men, shooting as he went. Following Stockton's example, the second outlaw did the same.

Taken completely by surprise, the three riders were unable to respond before they were all killed. Reining up momentarily, Stockton also shot and killed the three horses and two mules. This done, he and his partner raced for the mouth of the arroyo and on to Gallegos Canyon. The two outlaws, having mistaken the treasure hunters for lawmen, were completely unaware that they had just ridden past a million dollars' worth of gold ingots.

As the outlaws turned west after leaving the arroyo, the runoff that had accumulated in the high mountains several miles away was flowing in torrents into the adjacent drainage system. About an hour later, the arroyo was inundated by a raging flash flood, a three-foot-high wall of water washing over the path recently traveled by the fleeing gunmen.

The next morning, a short distance from the arroyo, two Mexican sheepherders, an old man and a boy, woke from their fitful sleep. The flimsy lean-to under which they had taken shelter had not offered much protection from the storm of the previous night, and one of the herders said he thought he heard gunshots sometime during the early morning.

After tending to the sheep, the older herder walked over to the rim of the arroyo and peered down into it. Nearly a foot of water still coursed along the sandy bottom, but it was not enough to cover the grisly remains of three men, their horses, and the pack mules. With the arrival of the second herder, the two men climbed down the steep bank of the arroyo and inspected the dead men and animals. Opening one of the leather packs still tied to a mule, the old man withdrew what he believed to be a long, heavy bar of iron. Curious, he opened all of the other packs and dumped dozens of the heavy bars onto the ground as he searched for anything valuable. Finding nothing, the two herders climbed back to the top of the arroyo and returned to their sheep. The old man carried one of the heavy bars with him and placed it among his belongings in the camp. An hour later the rains came again and continued into the night. That evening as the two herders fought for sleep under their leaky shelter, the arroyo was once again the scene of a violent flash flood, this one nearly ten feet deep, surging and crashing along the bottom, sweeping away everything in its path.

The next day Dolores Cancino, the owner of the sheep, arrived with supplies for his herders and learned of the tragedy in the arroyo from the old man. While telling the story, the herder handed Cancino the long ingot, which the sheepman immediately recognized as gold.

Leaving the boy to watch over the sheep, Cancino and the old man returned to the arroyo. Surprisingly, when they looked into the narrow chasm, it was still filled with muddy water from late arriving runoff. From wall to wall the muddy stream rushed through the channel. Cancino stayed the night with the herders and the next morning returned to the arroyo. The flood waters had receded, but during the night the men and animals had washed away.

For several hours Cancino rode along the rim, searching the arroyo bottom for their remains. Finally, he discovered one of the horses half-buried in sand. Diligent searching along the bottom of the muddy wash yielded the two remaining horses, but the bodies of the three men and the bars of gold were missing.

Several days later, Cancino traveled to Santa Fe, where he had the ingot assayed. He was delighted to learn that it contained a large percentage of gold and was cast in a style unique to the early Spanish miners. Cancino sold the ingot for four thousand dollars.

For several months, Cancino regularly searched the floor of the arroyo in the hope that subsquent flood waters would uncover some of the gold bars, but he found nothing.

The following year, Cancino met a man named Steve Upholt, a veteran gold miner who had made and lost several small fortunes during the previous twenty years. After telling Upholt the story of the gold bars in the arroyo, the miner became intrigued and provided Cancino some hope that the gold was likely still in the same location where the herders originally found it, but that it had probably settled several feet below the surface. Upholt explained to the sheepman that when thick deposits of loosely consolidated sands found in the bottom of an arroyo become saturated with water such as happens during a flood, they expand and become quite unstable, turning into quicksand. Anything of significant weight lying on top of these saturated sands, such as a bar of gold, would quickly sink to some depth below the surface. This, according to Upholt, was what happened to the gold ingots.

Forming a partnership, Cancino provided Upholt with directions to the arroyo. Several weeks later, the miner arrived in the area and, staying in the sheepherder's camp, spent many days exploring up and down the erosional feature. Since the killing of the three men two years earlier, several subsequent flash floods had occurred which modified the arroyo somewhat. In some places walls had caved in, in others tons of deposition of sand and debris had accumulated, and Upholt was fearful that the gold was buried much deeper than he originally believed. The configuration of the arroyo had changed so much that even Cancino's old sheepherder could not remember the exact point from the rim where he had first discovered the bodies of the men, mules, and horses.

One day while searching along the bottom of the arroyo, Upholt discovered a skeleton partially exposed along one bank. Exhuming it from the surrounding debris, he noted it was still partially clothed in rotting fragments of denim and wore a cartridge belt with a holster still containing a pistol. Believing the body to be that of one of the three men, and that it had been washed some distance down the arroyo from where the gold ingots were dumped, Upholt began to search upstream. The next day he found a second skeleton and, after examining it, discovered several of the ribs had been shattered, probably from a bullet.

Three days later, several yards upstream from the previous discovery, the third skeleton was found.

Upholt reasoned that the men, being lighter than the mules and horses, had been carried farther downstream by the flood waters. If he continued to search upstream, he should, with any luck at all, find the remains of the animals, and this would place him closer to the site at which the gold had been emptied from the leather panniers.

Another week passed and Upholt found the skeleton of one of the mules. A pack saddle and a rotted leather sack, likely used for carrying the gold, was also discovered nearby. At this point, Upholt believed he was close to the site where the bars had been dumped, for above the rim and a short distance away was the camp of the sheepherders. Selecting a likely spot, Upholt began to dig.

The work was tedious, but the miner was convinced that persistence would pay off. Upholt excavated three holes along the floor of the arroyo, each of them in excess of six feet in depth. Using a probe, he determined the depth of bedrock and concluded the channel was covered in soft, loose sands to a depth of fifteen feet.

During the excavation of the fourth hole, Upholt found one of the gold bars. It lay approximately six and a half feet below the surface, evidence that his theory of heavier objects sinking into the sand was correct. Realizing he had discovered the approximate site at which the ingots were dumped, he resumed his digging with renewed enthusiasm, and found two more gold ingots during the next two days.

When Cancino arrived several days later, Upholt showed him what he had found. The following day, the two men left for Santa Fe, where they cashed in the gold and split the money. Upholt told Cancino that he needed to ride up to Colorado and check on one of his mining interests and would return in a month to dig for more of the gold ingots. The miner rode away that afternoon and, oddly, never returned.

Several months later Cancino decided to dig for the gold ingots himself and traveled to the arroyo. As before, flash floods had once again changed the appearance of the channel and filled in holes dug by Upholt.

Discouraged, Cancino abandoned the region and never again attempted to search for the gold. He eventually sold his sheep herd and retired to Santa Fe, where he purchased a small grocery store.

The remote, sandy wash, now known locally as Cancino's Arroyo, is occasionally visited by modern-day treasure hunters who continue to search for the ingots. The gold, worth well over a million dollars today, has likely settled even deeper into the soft sands, farther and farther away from the probing shovels and metal detectors of the treasure hunters.

Lost Treasure of the Lava Beds

Dust rose in thick swirls above the slow-moving pack train as it wound its way single file along the ancient Indian trail. Other than the braying of mules, the only sounds that could be heard were the cracks of the whips and the cursing of the drivers.

The year was 1770, and the leader of the train was an officer in the Spanish military who had been given the assignment of escorting the huge cargo of silver ingots carried by the mules to Mexico City. This was his third journey along this route, a narrow, twisting, tortuous path that traversed a large section of the desert Southwest. Previous expeditions in this area always yielded evidence of Indians, but none was ever seen. This time, however, the officer could not shake the feeling that something bad was about happen. His concerns grew as he realized that the pack train was about to enter a narrow passageway through a portion of the hostile lava beds.

The men and animals had been on the trail for nearly three weeks. After leaving the rich silver mines near what is now Durango, Colorado, they had experienced torrential rains, flood-swollen streams, and severe sandstorms that reduced visibility to zero. The bad weather finally ceased as they approached the vast lava beds south of Grants, New Mexico; however, rather than being encouraged, the men appeared tentative, almost fearful. Even the mules seemed to be jumpy and nervous as, one by one, they entered the cramped passageway called the Narrows. Fourteen of the mules each carried three hundred pounds of silver ingots, packed tightly in leather panniers. Another half dozen transported food and supplies. The officer knew this passageway well and recalled that it continued for about a hundred yards before opening into a wide, flat, grassy meadow. Beyond the meadow was the entrance to another long, narrow passageway that eventually exited into the wide open plains to the south. Once out of the second canyon, the officer opined, the pack train would be safe.

As the last mule entered the Narrows, it was followed by two herders who brought up the rear. After several seconds had elapsed, about two dozen Indians rose from their places of concealment in the adjacent lava beds and entered the passageway, effectively sealing off any retreat by the Spaniards.

As the pack train entered the open, grassy meadow at the end of the Narrows, the officer ordered a temporary halt. He instructed the herders to unpack the animals and stack the loads under a high rock overhang in the shade. As the soldiers and herders sat on the packs and drank water from their canteens, the animals were turned loose to graze. The officer was lifting a canteen to his lips when he saw several Indians fill the entrance to the southern passageway. Looking behind him, his fear rose as he discovered more Indians pouring out of the narrow defile they had just passed through. On either side of the meadow, the high, steep walls of the rugged lava beds surrounded the meadow, preventing escape.

For nearly an hour the two opposing forces regarded each other from a distance, each assessing the relative strength of the other. Suddenly and without warning, several Indians began shooting arrows into the throng of Spaniards, wounding two. In retaliation, the Spaniards raised and fired their heavy muskets at the Indians, killing several. Within seconds, the Indians disappeared into the narrow passageways.

As the Spanish officer pondered the few options at his disposal, several Indians appeared on the rim above the grassy meadow and fired arrows into the massed and confused newcomers. Quickly retreating under the overhang, the Spaniards were safe from attack but were unable to return fire.

For several days, the Spaniards huddled under the protection of the rock as the Indians guarded the escape routes. Once in a while a herder or soldier would run out into the open and attempt to fire a shot at the Indians on the rim, but more often than not, he was pierced by arrows.

On the evening of the third day of hiding under the protective overhang, the officer decided the only way to escape from the lava beds was to fight their way out. Not wanting to be encumbered by the thousands of pounds of silver, he ordered the ingots buried. Several of the herders dug a long trench into which the silver was placed and then covered up. This done, the officer walked to the wall of the overhang and painstakingly scratched the image of a coiled snake into the weathered basalt. The serpent was a traditional Spanish symbol often used to indicate the presence of buried treasure.

On the fourth day, the officer noted the food supplies were beginning to run low. Realizing they could not hold out much longer, the frustrated Spaniards grabbed up their firearms and ran toward the southern passageway, determined to fight their way out of the enclosed meadow. Almost immediately, several of them were killed by arrows fired by the Indians on the rim. When the few remaining Spaniards reached the entrance to the narrow canyon, they were immediately slaughtered by the Indians they encountered there. Within minutes, every last Spaniard was scalped and hacked to pieces.

Taking the surviving horses and mules, the Indians left the meadow through the northern canyon, completely uninterested in the incredible cache of silver buried under the rock overhang.

Many years passed, and the bones of the dead Spaniards were gnawed by rodents and scattered and carried away by larger animals, until nothing but a few pieces of their armor remained, rusting on the floor of the meadow.

More time passed, and white settlers began to move into the area of western New Mexico. It wasn't long before cattlemen discovered the grassy meadow in the lava beds and grazed their livestock on it. Occasionally, a rancher or cowhand would discover a piece of rusted Spanish armor, but none was aware of the rich treasure in silver ingots buried nearby under the rock overhang.

One of the ranchers, a man named Solomon Bilbo, married an Acoma Indian woman and learned from her the tale of the massacre of the Spaniards in the meadow. Though the tale was clouded from being handed down through several generations, part of the legend suggested the Spaniards were transporting a great load of silver from the mines in Colorado to Mexico City when they were attacked and killed. Bilbo, intrigued by the tale, searched long and hard for the treasure, but as there were several high rock overhangs surrounding the meadow, he had difficulty locating the cache and finally gave up.

One day during the 1930s, a young Indian arrived at the York Ranch in western New Mexico. He carried with him an old map which purported to show the location of the buried silver in the lava beds. According to the legend, said the Indian, the Spanish officer sketched the map just before he was killed. While searching the dead bodies following the slaughter, a warrior had discovered the map and, intrigued by the strange symbols, kept it. The map was passed down through several generations of the warrior's descendants until it eventually fell into the possession of the young Indian. Prominently displayed on the map, apparently pointing to the location of the silver cache, was the image of a coiled snake.

With the help of several ranch hands, the Indian conducted a search of the grassy meadow in the lava beds, but found nothing. Apparently the searchers never noticed the coiled snake etched into one wall of the canyon.

Several years later when the tale of the lost treasure had faded from the memories of the area residents, a young cowhand rode into the York Ranch headquarters seeking treatment for a severe rattlesnake bite. As he was lying in bed with a high fever from the toxic venom, the ranch foreman asked him where the incident occurred. The cowhand, growing weaker, told him it happened in the grassy meadow in the lava beds, in the shade of the overhang that had an image of a snake carved into the wall.

Recalling the old tale of buried Spanish treasure, the foreman decided to search for the inscription. Riding out the next morning, he explored all around the meadow but was unable to locate the carving. When he returned to the ranch that evening, he sought the cowhand to obtain better directions only to learn the unfortunate youth had died from his snakebite.

Today, the search for the lost Spanish treasure of the lava beds continues. Although at least three well-equipped expeditions have explored the grassy meadow seeking the cache, the fourteen mule loads of silver remain hidden.

Madame Barcelo's Lost $500,000 in Gold Coins

Raul Cortez was one of the best-known packers and transporters in the Rocky Mountain West during the 1830s. With his partner, Manuel DeGrazi, Cortez contracted for and delivered goods from as far north as Montana, as far east as Missouri, and south into Mexico. His reputation of competency, efficiency, and trustworthiness placed him in great demand among those needing to ship goods and articles of great value. After several years as a successful packer and businessman, Cortez began to limit his clientele to the wealthy and powerful, and he was paid handsomely for his services.

During the spring of 1839, Cortez and DeGrazi, both Spaniards, arrived in Santa Fe along with three Mexican helpers to deliver a pack train laden with goods for a growing mercantile operation. While the men were resting up from their long journey, Cortez was summoned to the office of the governor of the territory. Governor Manuel Armijo introduced the well-known packer to one Madame Barcelo, who, the governor told Cortez, had need of his services.

Madame Barcelo, who real name was Maria Toulos, operated a successful gambling casino-saloon-bordello in Santa Fe, and during the previous few months had amassed a fortune in gold coins from traders, trappers, settlers, and soldiers who patronized her establishment. Because the few banks that had been established in Santa Fe at this time provided little or no security and were generally run by men of questionable character, Madame Barcelo chose to ship her gold to an established bank in New York. She informed Cortez she wished to employ him to deliver five hundred thousand dollars' worth of gold coins to Independence, Missouri, where it would be loaded onto a paddlewheel, sent on to New Orleans where it would be transferred to a steamer, and then shipped to New York.

Cortez cautioned Madame Barcelo that the route between Santa Fe and Independence was filled with Indians and bandits, and that the journey was likely to be frought with difficulty. Madame Barcelo advised Cortez to employ a dozen well-armed guards to accompany her fortune and that she would pay for them, but he demurred. A large number of guards, he explained to her, suggested to potential bandits that the pack train carried something of value. The fewer men involved, he claimed, the more insignificant the pack train would appear.

Following more discussion, Cortez finally agreed to accept the cargo, and made plans to load the gold and depart early the next morning. The gold was stuffed into twenty-four stout leather panniers and tied securely to twelve strong mules. Cortez learned early in his packing career that mules were far more dependable than wagons for transporting goods. The durable and sure-footed animals were able to negotiate steep, narrow mountain passes with little difficulty, and rarely became ill.

When the mules were finally loaded and supplies for the journey purchased and packed, Cortez, DeGrazi, and the three helpers led the caravan out of Santa Fe toward the northeast, following a well-traveled trail into the Sangre de Cristo Mountains.

Around midday, one of the packers riding at the rear of the single-file mule train notified Cotez they were being followed. The packer and Cortez rode to high ground and spotted ten riders about a mile away. Cortez recommended they continue to drive the mules onward and keep an eye on the men behind them.

That evening as Cortez's party settled into camp, guards were posted. Around midnight, one of the guards informed Cortez that a group of ten men had just passed by the camp on the north side, heading in the general direction traveled by the mule train. The guard told Cortez they were Mexicans, and all were well armed.

The next morning as the mules were loaded, Cortez warned his men of the possibility of an ambush somewhere on the trail ahead. It was a tense and wary group that rode along that morning, carefully scanning the hills and woods. Approximately forty miles east of Taos, Cortez's pack train was attacked. Surging out of a nearby gully, the bandits advanced on the mule train, firing wildy as they went. Cortez immediately led his men and mules into a jumble of large rocks and took shelter, and for the rest of the day the two opposing groups exchanged gunfire. Cortez left the gold packed onto the mules, for he did not know when he might be able to seize an opportunity to escape from the confines of the rocks.

During a brief lull in the gun battle, Cortez noted that the site in which they took shelter consisted of an irregular circle of several large, weathered rocks. Three huge boulders, each twice the size of a two-story house, dominated the site.

When darkness arrived, the attackers crept onto the large rocks overlooking the defenders and positioned themselves in such a way that when the sun rose in the morning, they would be able to pick them off one by one. With the first light, the firing commenced and DeGrazi, who was caught in the open tending to one of the mules, was killed immediately. Seconds later, one of the helpers was shot through the head and was dead before his body struck the ground.

Cortez and the other two helpers drove the mules under a nearby overhanging boulder and took up defensive positions. While they were thus out of sight of the attackers, Cortez ordered the helpers to dig a trench in which to bury their companions. As the two men were lowered into the shallow grave, Cortez was seized by an idea. Instructing the men to enlarge the trench, he began unpacking the gold from the mules. As the trench grew, Cortez placed the leather panniers filled with gold coins into it. When the last of them was deposited, the trench was filled in with dirt and a fire built over it.

With the five hundred thousand dollars in gold coins adequately hidden, Cortez felt it prudent to surrender to the attackers, try to convince them they were transporting nothing of value, and hope they would allow them to continue their journey. Once away from the bandits, Cortez reasoned, they could return for Madame Barcelo's gold.

Cortez sent one of the packers to the top of a large boulder to wave a white kerchief and request a discussion with the bandit leader. The man was immediately shot and killed, and Cortez and the remaining packer sunk deeper into the protective recess of their hiding place.

Around sundown, the bandit leader, calling from a nearby hiding place, asked to be allowed to approach. When Cortez agreed to the request, the bandit informed him that if he would relinquish the gold he and his remaining helper would be allowed to go free. Cortez denied any knowledge of gold, but the bandit leader told him he knew all about the shipment of coins consigned to him by Madame Barcelo. Cortez continued to deny he possessed any gold, but while he was thus engaged in discussion with the bandit, several others crept up behind him, leveled their rifles at his head, and ordered him to drop his guns. Cortez carefully placed his guns on the ground and stepped back a few paces, but at this point the remaining packer decided to attempt an escape. Before he could cover twenty yards, however, he was shot dead.

The bandit leader commanded his followers to search the area for the coins, and as the outlaws fanned out looking for the gold, Cortez calmly placed a pot of coffee on the fire to boil.

Frustrated at not finding the gold after a thorough search, the Mexican leader decided that Cortez was telling the truth. The bandits were all for killing the packer until one of them recognized him as the brother of Father Cortez, a highly respected priest in New Mexico. Instead, they took him prisoner, tied him to a horse, and rode away.

For the next three weeks, the bandits rode south into Mexico. While the leader originally believed taking Cortez prisoner was a good idea, he now regretted having an extra mouth to feed. Because the bandits gradually grew unconcerned about their prisoner, Cortez was no longer tied or guarded, and fed only what the other men were unable to eat. One night as the rest of the camp slept, the Spaniard stole a horse and rode away into the night. A few days later he arrived at the Rio Grande and followed it northward, knowing it would eventually lead to Santa Fe.

The journey was a difficult one for Cortez. Although he was trail-hardened from many years of traveling and living in the wilderness, he was weak from the poor diet provided by his Mexican captors. In addition to malnutrition, he was suffering from dysentery. For several days he rode through driving rainstorms and suffered cold, shivering, and fever. As he had no weapons he was unable to shoot game and lived on a meager diet of lizards, grasshoppers, and berries. Nearly a month after his escape from the bandits, Cortez finally arrived at the outskirts of Santa Fe. Terribly emaciated, sick, and weakened from the hard journey, the Spaniard collapsed from his horse and was found the next day by a passing horseman and taken into the city.

After he was identified, Cortez was carried to the dwelling of Madame Barcelo where he was provided a private room in which to recover. While he was being ministered

142

to by a physician, Cortez explained to Madame Barcelo what had transpired since his party had left Santa Fe two months earlier. He assured her that her fortune in gold coins was safely buried in the mountains east of Taos. Still weak from his ordeal, Cortez sketched a crude map showing the three large rocks where he and his party took cover from the attacking bandits. On the map he drew the location of the trench near one of the rocks where the half million dollars in gold coins were buried. Weakened from this effort, Cortez fell back on his pillow and told Madame Barcelo that as soon as he recovered he would lead an expedition to the three rocks and retrieve her treasure for her.

The next afternoon, Raul Cortez died.

Within a few days, Madame Barcelo, with the help of Santa Fe Mayor Louis Robidoux, organized a party of men to travel to the region of the three large rocks, dig up the gold, and return it to Santa Fe. Madame Barcelo gave the leader of the group the map drawn by Cortez, a decision she was to later regret.

After ten days had passed and the men had not returned, the mayor organized another party to search for them. Along the trail about twenty-five miles northeast of Santa Fe, the original party was found, all killed, scalped, and mutilated. All of their personal effects had been taken. The map drawn by Cortez, the only directions to the lost gold, could not be found.

The twenty-four packs filled with gold coins most assuredly still lie buried somewhere in the foothills of the Sangre de Cristo Mountain range. The irregular circle of rocks, dominated by three huge boulders, has eluded searchers for more than 150 years.

Lost Train Robbery Loot in Cibola County

Just after sundown on November 6, 1897, the Santa Fe Railroad evening train pulled into the station in Grants to take on fuel and water before continuing eastward. As fireman Henry Abel jumped from the engine onto the loading platform, a man stepped from the shadows with a drawn revolver and shoved the end of the barrel into the face of the terrified railroader, commanding him to reboard. As Abel climbed back into the engine, H.D. McCarty, the engineer, fled out the opposite side. Seconds later, the sound of gunfire confirmed what Abel suspected—the train was being robbed.

As passengers were being relieved of their valuables, the gunman, still holding the pistol to Abel's head, ordered the fireman to release the air brakes and move the train about a mile down the track. A few minutes later, with the lights of Grants in the distance, all but the baggage, mail, and express cars were detached and the train proceeded another two miles before stopping.

As Abel watched, two more gunmen, seemingly appearing out of the darkness, advanced on the express car. Several minutes passed as they affixed a charge of explosives to the locked sliding door. Finally, it was set off, and the entire side of the boxcar blew apart. Anyone who might have been inside guarding the cargo had long since departed, so the robbers entered the destroyed car in search of the safe that was normally transported on this particular run. After finding a steel Wells-Fargo safe, another charge was set and a foot-wide opening was blown into it. As the smoke cleared, the outlaws removed more than one hundred thousand dollars in gold and silver coins and currency.

Quickly, the bandits stuffed the money into saddlebags, loaded them onto spare horses, and rode away. As fireman Abel watched the outlaws escape into the distance, the leader stopped, turned back toward him, and announced that Black Jack had struck again. As Abel pondered this cryptic information, the robbers rode due south into the rugged and forbidding lava beds that were frequently the hiding place of bandits and renegade Indians.

After the train returned to Grants and the robbery was reported, a special force composed of Wells-Fargo agents, railroad officials, the county sheriff, and several deputies was assembled to pursue the bandits. For two days the posse searched throughout the lava beds but never encountered the robbers. At one point, the lawmen were within a hundred yards of the outlaws' hiding place but failed to pick up the trail.

Although a large reward was offered, no information on the train robbers ever came forth. The authorities concluded the gang was led by the notorious Black Jack Christian, but no trace of the outlaws was ever found.

Following the successful robbery of the train, Black Jack Christian led his two companions to a favorite campsite some twenty miles south of Grants. Formerly an old Indian campground, the low, sheltered break in the surrounding volcanic rock offered protection against the harsh desert winds, had a good spring of fresh water nearby, and afforded a defensible position against pursuing lawmen. As they prepared to spend the night, the outlaws opened bottles of whiskey and celebrated their newly acquired wealth. Before an hour passed, all became quite drunk.

As will often happen when a group of men are drinking, a fight broke out. One of Christian's companions, enraged at a comment made by the other, pulled a gun and shot the offender through the head, killing him instantly. As the two remaining outlaws scooped a hole out of the soft ground in which to bury the dead man, Christian heard the sounds of men riding in the distance. Cautioning his companion to remain quiet, Christian moved cat-like to a nearby rise in the lava beds and spotted the posse about two hundred yards away. The lawmen had evidently heard the sound of the earlier gunshot, but appeared confused as to which direction it had come from. Quickly, Christian returned to the campsite and informed the other outlaw of the proximity of the posse. To lighten their load while making an escape, Christian pulled the money-filled saddlebags from the horses and threw them into the open grave. After placing the body of the dead outlaw on top of the loot, the grave was filled and the two men mounted up and rode away to the south and out of the lava beds.

When they believed they had completely eluded the posse, Christian suggested the two split up and ride in different directions. The outlaws agreed to meet in thirty days at a specified location and return together to the lava beds to dig up the money and divide it.

Within the month, however, Christian was killed near Silver City during a holdup attempt, and his companion was tracked down and arrested following an aborted train robbery in Arizona. He died years later in the Yuma Territorial Prison.

Before Christian perished from the gunshot wounds received during his final robbery attempt, he told lawmen of burying the one hundred thousand dollars in gold and silver coins and currency in the lava beds south of Grants. Though he provided detailed directions to the location, several expeditions into the area failed to locate the site. Search parties usually became lost and returned frustrated.

Several years later, a cowboy wandering through the vast lava beds south of Grants chanced upon a low, dirt-covered depression. Because the location was out of the wind and a decent freshwater spring was close by, he decided to camp there for the night. As he sat by his campfire sipping coffee, he noticed a small, weathered mound of dirt not far away. Upon examining it, he wondered if someone might have buried a treasure at this location sometime in the past. After excavating a few inches of soil, however, he came upon a shriveled corpse and quickly refilled the hole. Had the cowboy only removed the body, he would have discovered an incredible fortune packed in old leather saddlebags just beneath it. Years later, the cowboy learned the story of the Grants train robbery and the burial of the loot. Convinced he had accidentally discovered the cache the night he camped in the lava beds, he spent several months attempting to relocate the campsite.

He never found it, and the money from the Santa Fe Railroad train robbery still lies buried beneath a few inches of dirt in a hidden recess of the lava beds, guarded by the skeleton of a dead outlaw.

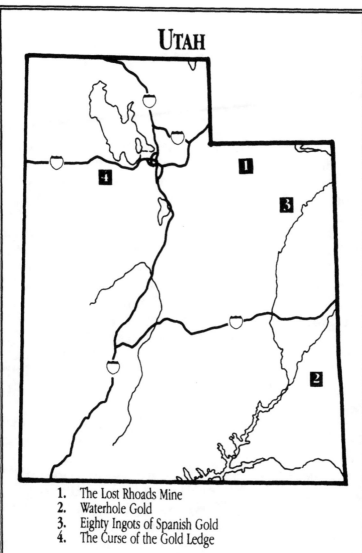

UTAH

1. The Lost Rhoads Mine
2. Waterhole Gold
3. Eighty Ingots of Spanish Gold
4. The Curse of the Gold Ledge

The Lost Rhoads Mines

During much of the Spanish reign over a large portion of the American West, gold and silver mining involving hundreds of Spaniards, Mexicans, and Indian slaves was conducted in various locations throughout the Rocky Mountains. The extracted ore was normally smelted at some location near the mine, fashioned into ingots, and then transported hundreds of miles south to Mexico City, the seat of the government at the time. Here the precious metal was inventoried and shipped overland to the East Coast, where it was loaded onto ships and sailed to Spain to fill the treasury of the motherland.

While mining ore in the Rocky Mountains, the Spaniards generally did so in opposition to the wishes of the local Indians. In many cases, the Indians were simply conquered and enslaved to work in the mines. In other cases, they were evicted from the region or killed. Occasionally, however, the Spaniards encountered Indians who refused to be dominated by the newcomers and fought back.

Dozens of mines were operated by the Spanish in the Uinta Mountains of northeastern Utah. The Uintas proved to be a rich location, and in time hundreds of Spaniards were assigned to the region to oversee the extraction of thousands of pounds of gold and silver annually. Government officials in Mexico City looked with favor upon the wealthy and productive mines of the Uintas and eagerly anticipated the gold- and silver-laden pack trains that delivered the wealth from the north country several times a year.

On first entering the Uintas, the Spaniards encountered some early resistance from the Ute Indians who resided there. Many of these Indians were captured, enslaved, and put to work in the mines. Those who escaped capture by the Spaniards conducted a savage warfare with the newcomers at every opportunity, and life for the European miners in the Uinta Mountains was far from safe and secure.

As the Spaniards conducted their mining activities, the Utes preyed on them ruthlessly. When Spanish hunting parties went out into the mountains to obtain game, Utes attacked and killed them. Occasionally, Indians would perch on nearby ridges and lob arrows into the Spanish camp, killing several of its members.

Each year as winter approached, the Spaniards closed up the mines and returned to Mexico with their accumulated bullion. In the warmer climate far to the south they would rest and await the spring thaws, at which time they would return to the mountains and resume excavating the ore.

In mid-autumn of 1680, as the snows began to fall and the temperature dropped precipitously, several mines in the heart of the Uinta Mountains were closed down for the winter season. The accumulated gold ingots were loaded into stout leather pouches and tied firmly to burros. As the long pack train bound for Mexico City wound slowly down a steep mountain trail and entered a broad meadow, the party of Spaniards was suddenly attacked by nearly a hundred Utes who came streaming out of the nearby forest. Not anticipating such an offensive, the Spaniards were caught by surprise and, completely unprepared for battle, all perished in the subsequent slaughter.

When the final Spaniard was slain, the Indians loaded their victims onto the burros and horses and, turning the pack train around, led them back up the mountain toward the mines. Once there, they dumped the ingots into a deep shaft along with the bodies of the dead men. They then covered the entrances to the mines and left them as a symbol of the white man's greed.

Many years later, a large party of Mormons arrived at what is now Salt Lake City, located just to the west of the Uinta Mountains. Led by Brigham Young, the Mormons believed that American Indians were descended from the lost tribe of Israel and, as a result, showed the Utes some respect, treatment they had received from no other whites they had ever encountered. Young's motivations went beyond mere religious considerations, however, for he believed if he patronized the local Indians and treated them fairly the new settlers would be less likely to suffer from theft of livestock and occasional raids.

Within a few years, Salt Lake City grew to be a thriving community located along the path of many westbound wagon trains. Commerce was brisk as travelers bought and traded for goods they needed.

Many of the Salt Lake City merchants insisted that payment for goods be made with gold. Present during one such transaction was a Ute Indian chief named Yahkira who remained fascinated with the white man's use of the ore as a bartering tool.

Several weeks later, Chief Yahkira visited Brigham Young and showed him several large gold nuggets. Yahkira, who was called Chief Walker by the Mormons, told Young that because his people had been friendly toward the Utes he would take him to a place where the gold could be found in abundance. Realizing the need for gold in his growing community, Young agreed to accompany Yahkira, and the next morning found the two riding eastward toward the heart of the Uinta Mountains, some ninety miles away.

As Young and Chief Yahkira slowly made their way up a twisting mountain trail, the Indian related the tale of the Indian attack on the Spanish pack train and the subsequent hiding of the gold along with the bodies of the Spanish soldiers. He explained to the Mormon how the Indians were protective of their mountain stronghold and resented the encroachment of whites into the area. While showing Young the location of several rich gold mines, the Indian exacted a promise from him never to reveal the secret location except to those whom the Mormon leader personally designated to travel to the mountains and retrieve the gold from the mines.

In 1853, a man named Thomas Rhoads arrived at Salt Lake City. Rhoads was a devout Mormon and a qualified surveyor and miner who had made a fortune in the California gold fields. Now a rich man, he felt a need to commit himself more fully to the church. Young was aware of Rhoads's experience as a miner and summoned him to his chambers, where he informed him of the existence of the old Spanish gold mines in the Uinta Mountains and of the church's need for the ore.

Taking an oath never to reveal the location of the rich mines, Rhoads, in the company of several Indian guides, was led into the remote interior of the mountain range. Ten days later he returned to Salt Lake City leading a pack mule heavily loaded with gold nuggets. Rhoads stated many years later that using only his own two hands he had been able to pick up enough large nuggets and flakes of gold to fill a pair of saddlebags without ever moving from one spot. The supply of raw gold, he said, was inexhaustible! Thomas Rhoads made dozens of trips into the Uinta Mountains over the next several years.

The secret of the location of the rich gold mines remained soley with Young and Rhoads and a handful of Utes. The last thing leader Young wanted was a gold rush into his growing Mormon state of Deseret. Quietly, he ordered the construction of a small smelter and mint and began to produce gold coins to be used by his followers. In addition, much of the gold that was brought into Salt Lake City by Rhoads was fashioned into artifacts which to this day adorn the Mormon temple in Salt Lake City.

Occasionally when Rhoads would slip into the Uinta Mountains to retrieve some gold he would take along his young son, Caleb. While the boy never swore an oath of secrecy, the Indians tolerated his presence in the mountains because of his youth. As Caleb grew older, however, he began to appreciate the value of gold and, when he was able to get away with it, would slip alone into the mountains and take some gold for himself.

Years went by and Brigham Young and Thomas Rhoads both passed away. After the death of the elder Rhoads in 1869, Caleb was chosen by the church to continue his father's work of retrieving the gold from the Uinta Mountains and delivering it to the Mormon leaders. It was a position Caleb was to hold for many years to come. Aside from just a few Indians, Caleb Rhoads was the only man who knew the location of the fabulously rich gold mines.

Whether Caleb was paid handsomely by the Mormon church for his efforts in retrieving the gold or whether he simply kept some of the ore for himself will never be known, but over the years he prospered, became a successful landowner and cattle rancher, and until his dying day was one of the wealthiest men in the state of Utah.

Caleb Rhoads died on June 2, 1905, and with his passing also went the knowledge of the location of the secret gold mines. During his final days, Caleb actually attempted to communicate some information about the mines, but his descriptions were cryptic and the only map he ever sketched was impossible to interpret.

Unlike his father, Caleb had never sworn an oath to keep secret the location of the mines. Also unlike his father, he did not feel a particularly strong obligation to the Mormon church. Rhoads, as he grew older and less able to travel into the mountains, tried several times to inform others of the location of the mines. A few tried to follow his directions, but once in the mountains the searchers became disoriented and lost.

And there have been many searchers. Once news of the extensive gold deposits in the Uintas became widespread, prospectors arrived in the area in droves to try to strike it rich. A few apparently found gold, but many more found only death.

Sometime during the 1890s, two hard-rock prospectors who had spent a great deal of time in the Uinta Mountains searching for the Rhoads Mines were seen leaving the area leading two mules transporting heavy packs. Once out of the mountains, they stopped at the ranch of a man they knew to water their horses and, while engaging in conversation, showed the rancher their packs full of gold. The rancher reported that the two prospectors made several other trips into the mountains, each time returning with impressive cargos of ore. When asked, the two men remained secretive, claiming only that they had located the same gold deposits from which Rhoads had obtained his ore.

The two prospectors were last seen riding into the mountains one spring to bring out yet another rich load of gold, but they never returned. It was later rumored they were killed by Ute Indians who allegedly still guarded the gold deep in the mountains.

In 1956, a hunter named Clark Rhoads may have accidentally found one of the gold mines known to his namesake. While deer hunting in the Uinta Mountains one winter, Rhoads found a set of bobcat tracks in the snow and followed them to an old mine shaft. Having no flashlight, Rhoads decided not to enter the old mine at the time. He returned the following summer, however, explored the shaft, and discovered several Spanish mining artifacts. He noted that the shaft had been filled in and was curious why anyone would go to so much trouble. Intrigued by the color of some of the rocks he found on the floor of the mines, he pocketed several. Later, when he had them assayed, they proved to have a heavy gold content. Rhoads made no attempt to excavate the fill from the mine for he feared the unstable rock structure would collapse at any time.

Many others have found gold in the Uintas. During the autumn of 1988, two sixteen-year-old Ute Indian boys were found to be in possession of six ingots of gold. The ingots were of the style and size preferred by the Spaniards and, in fact, two of them had Spanish letters and symbols engraved on them. When questioned, the boys told authorities the bars were taken from a large cache containing many similar ingots, but they were afraid to provide any more information for fear they would be killed by members of their tribe.

It may be so. Legend persists that the Ute Indians still guard and protect these mountains and the gold and silver that are found therein. Many who have entered the deep and remote parts of these mountains have been killed, usually shot from a distance. There are records of over two dozen unsolved and unexplained murders in the gold-filled Uinta Mountains.

Are the Indians still guarding the gold? It would seem so.

Waterhole Gold

During the middle of the nineteenth century, hundreds of settlers, miners, trappers, hunters, outlaws, and others simply in need of a change or a challenge traveled across the country and into the promise of the American West. They sought land, wealth, adventure, a new beginning. During these long journeys, travelers often found it necessary to stop and trade for or purchase supplies along the way. At a remote trading post in eastern Utah, migrants often observed Snake Indians who came from their distant camps to buy goods and always payed with gold nuggets of the purest quality. Travelers often remarked at the buckskin pouches carried by the Indians, heavy with gold and dangling from a cord around their necks. One settler wrote a letter to a relative back East about the abundance and quality of the Snake Indian gold, a letter that was found many years later and which initiated the search for and discovery of a rich deposit of placer gold in eastern Utah.

Frank Lane had recently graduated from law school at Yale and was preparing to settle into a position with a law firm somewhere on the East Coast. He felt, however, that he should have one great adventure before turning his efforts toward office and courthouse work. Accidentally discovering the letter referring to the Snake Indian gold sometime in the 1880s, Lane decided he would travel to the West the following spring and search for the source of this fabulous wealth. Lane invited Lawrence Kennedy, a resident of Boston and a former classmate of his, to accompany him. Kennedy agreed, and several weeks later the two were prospecting streams and searching for outcrops of gold in the Rocky Mountains along the Colorado-Utah border.

For months the two young men explored and prospected in the high mountains. They had the times of their lives camping and hunting in the clean mountain air and trading stories with trappers and scouts, but they found very little gold.

As winter approached, the men left the high country of the western Colorado Rockies and descended to the lower elevations of eastern Utah. Having no luck there, they moved on toward the drier lowlands. They continued to prospect along the way for ore but still had no luck finding gold.

Lane gradually grew discouraged with the search and became anxious to return to the East and make his mark in the law profession. He decided to turn all of his equipment over to Kennedy.

After Lane left, Kennedy continued to travel and prospect throughout eastern Utah, enjoying the wild and free life. From time to time he would encounter Snake Indians and from them he learned something of the origins of their gold.

Many years earlier, an elderly Snake Indian told Kennedy, the red men learned that whites craved the shiny mineral and in exchange for it would provide the Indians with guns, ammunition, blankets, and food. The Indians had long known that the mineral existed in great quantities in a wide gravel deposit near the foothills of the La Sal Mountains. The Indian told Kennedy the squaws dug into the gravel about two feet down where they would encounter numerous large nuggets lying atop a bedrock of sandstone.

Several weeks later, Kennedy was hunting some distance from his camp near the La Sal Mountains. He killed a deer and, on his way back to camp, stopped to get a drink from a waterhole he spied in a wide gravel wash. As he scooped up handfuls of water, he noticed small gleaming stones in profusion in the bottom of the pothole.

Stepping into the shallow pool, Kennedy reached down into the water and retrieved a small handful of gold nuggets! Elated with his discovery, he returned to his camp, cooked a portion of his kill, and spent a restless night. Before the sun rose the next morning, Kennedy was on his way to the waterhole, carrying a gold pan and a canvas ore sack. After pulling nuggets out of the waterhole for about two hours, Kennedy had completely filled the sack. Once it was full, he continued to retrieve nuggets, which he stuffed into his pockets.

The next day, on returning to the waterhole, Kennedy explored the gravel wash for a hundred yards upstream and downstream and found about a dozen more holes, all with gold at the bottom. For several weeks he continued to take gold from the holes, and when he had nothing else in which to carry the ore, he decided to abandon the area and return to his home in Boston with his fortune.

Arriving back in the East, Kennedy invested his new-found wealth into a series of enterprises, all of which failed. After seven years he was broke, and decided to return to the gravel wash near the La Sal Mountains in eastern Utah and retrieve more gold.

Kennedy journeyed to Moab, and from this settlement he purchased a pack mule and supplies and headed into the mountains. Much to his dismay and frustration, Kennedy became lost and disoriented and could not remember how to reach the gravel wash from which he had mined several hundred thousand dollars years earlier. For three weeks he searched throughout the region, but he eventually gave up and returned to Boston.

Geologists tell us that gold, being one of the heavier metals, will readily sink to the lowest possible level in a stream with a loosely consolidated and unstratified gravel bottom. It is likely that the gold, probably carried into the

wash for centuries by runoff, slowly yet inexhorably fil-
tered its way through nearly two feet of gravel to accumulate on a layer of sandstone bedrock where the Snake
Indians found it. It is possible that the entire wash may
contain millions of dollars' worth of gold, making it one
of the richest placer deposits in history.

During the 1930s and 1940s, cattle ranchers who frequented the area of the La Sal Mountains mentioned seeing
the dry gravelly wash and the numerous waterholes located
throughout, but when they attempted to return to the area
they were unable to locate it.

Since the days when the Snake Indians dug the holes
in the wash over a hundred years ago, it is reasonable to
assume that the frequent runoff that flows from the nearby
mountains has smoothed out and covered the shallow
excavations. If someone could somehow identify the
specific wash from which Lawrence Kennedy extracted a
fortune in gold nuggets, it would be a small matter of
removing the two foot thick layer of gravel and retrieving
the ore that has settled atop the bedrock.

Eighty Ingots of Spanish Gold

Several miles north of Duchesne City in northeastern Utah, the Duchesne River and Rock Creek form a confluence. Not far from this point is a wide area called Daniels Flat, and it was near this location that a small Spanish settlement thrived more than three hundred years ago. In this rugged and remote setting, the settlement stood on a slightly rolling plain, at one end of which was a local landmark called Treasure Hill.

The Spanish established missions throughout much of the West ostensibly to convert the Indians to Christianity. Whatever the official position of the Spanish government, the fact remained that the Spaniards enslaved hundreds of Indians to work in the rich gold and silver mines they discovered in the region. Not far from Daniels Flat were several such mines, and during the course of the first three years of the settlement, an incredible fortune in gold ore was excavated, fashioned into large, bulky ingots, and stored in a low, crudely constructed rock and mortar structure to await transportation to Mexico City.

Ute Indians who had escaped capture by the Spaniards constantly plagued this small Daniels Flat settlement. Occasional raids were launched, and now and then a soldier or settler was killed, but the Spanish perceived these Indians as little more than a nuisance that would eventually be eliminated.

One day, however, a small hunting party of Spaniards rode hurriedly into the camp and warned the others that a large force of Utes was massing behind a nearby ridge and preparing an attack. The official in charge, believing the Indians were after the gold ingots, ordered the heavy bars loaded onto burros and hastily transported to an empty mine shaft adjacent to Rock Creek. As the soldiers readied their weapons in anticipation of the imminent attack, Indian laborers unloaded the ingots from the burros, carried them into the shaft, and stacked them against the far wall of a large chamber.

As soon as the Indians had completed the job of hiding the gold, they were herded back into the compound. As the last one passed through the gate, more than a hundred Utes stormed out of the nearby forest, attacked the settlement, and slew all of the Spaniards. Eveything was burned or otherwise destroyed, and the slaves were freed and returned to their families. Caring nothing for gold, the Utes were completely uninterested in the huge deposit of ingots in the small shaft near the creek.

The legend of the Spanish settlement with its mines and gold ingots was passed down through successive generations. Many people traveled to Daniels Flat to search for the cache, but none were successful—at least not until 1969, when a treasure hunter named Royce Bullock came along.

Bullock believed that with persistence and luck he might be able to find the golden hoard. Because the Daniels Flat area was somehow under the jurisdiction of the Ute Tribal Council, he tried several times, unsuccessfully, to obtain permission to search for the fortune. After being turned down three times, Bullock decided to search covertly, exploring the area in the dark of night.

With Treasure Hill looming in the background, Bullock stalked across Daniels Flat carrying a flashlight and metal detector. During his searches he discovered the outlines of several old stone structures, which he believed were the remains of the old Spanish mission and its associated outbuildings and living quarters. Not many years earlier, area ranchers from this region discovered portions of several old Spanish ox carts nearby, along with some mining equipment, swords, and buckles.

One evening, Bullock's explorations took him to the bank of nearby Rock Creek. He paused and knelt down to take a drink of water. As he did so, he noticed a small opening farther upstream and on the opposite bank, its shadow looking ominous in the bright moonlight. Crossing the narrow stream, Bullock went to inspect the opening and found it choked with brush and debris. He pulled some of the material away, and soon uncovered an old mine shaft which extended back under the low hill bordering the stream.

Twisting several bunches of grass together to serve as torches, Bullock lit one and entered the dark shaft. Bullock crept for more than twenty-five yards along the low passageway until it opened up into a large chamber. As he examined the excavation, something against the far wall reflected the light of his torch. On closer inspection, Bullock discovered dozens of large gold bars, stacked like cordwood against the rock wall.

With his heart pounding heavily in his chest, Bullock counted eighty of the gold bars and tried to imagine what an incredible fortune they represented. When he tried to lift one of the large ingots, he was surprised to discover it took all of his strength. Bullock realized he would have to obtain help in order to remove the gold from the chamber.

Accompanied by a trusted friend, Bullock returned several times in the dark of night to the long-forgotten mine shaft. With great difficulty, the two men managed to remove two of the bars on each trip.

The day after their fourth clandestine venture into Daniels Flat, Bullock's partner suffered a heart attack and died. Bullock, satisfied with his take from the chamber, and fearful that some kind of curse might be attached to the gold, decided not to return.

In a moment of indiscretion several weeks later, Bullock let slip some information about his discovery, and others were soon searching the Daniels Flat area for the hidden Spanish treasure. The searchers immediately encountered two problems. First, most of them were summarily chased from the region by the Indian caretakers of the property. And secondly, since 1969 the channel of Rock Creek had changed somewhat, and at various points where it flows adjacent to Daniels Flat, tons of gravel had been deposited. One such deposition, it is believed, covered the entrance to the mine shaft that holds the remaining seventy-two bars of gold.

Perhaps the creek will change course again sometime in the future, exposing the opening that leads to millions of dollars in gold at the end of the shaft.

The Curse of the Gold Ledge

When Brigham Young led his hardy band of Mormons into the valley of the Great Salt Lake during the summer of 1847, he immediately realized the great promise of the land and the impending hardships his followers were certain to encounter during the course of settling it.

Aware that the ultimate survival of his flock depended on successful agriculture, Young assigned several men to begin breaking the ground and planting seed. While the familes lived temporarily in their wagons and in tents, another contingent of men was sent into the nearby forested canyons in order to determine the availability of timber and locate appropriate sites for establishing sawmills. Young was hopeful that, with diligence and hard work, adequate houses could be constructed before the cold of winter set in.

Young assigned John Rowberry to examine the foothills of the Black Rock Ridge south of the lake for a suitable location for a sawmill. A dependable stream with a consistent flow was necessary to power the saw blade, and Rowberry located one such site near what is now Twin Springs.

Rowberry supervised the construction of the sawmill and had it operating in a short time. Timber was hauled to the mill from the nearby canyons of Settlement and Middle, cut up into lumber, and transported to the various building locations in Salt Lake City and Tooele.

Several weeks following the opening of the sawmill, Rowberry suffered a serious accident and was confined to bed. Within a few days, Mormon leader Young designated a man named Croslin to take Rowberry's place. Croslin was a young sheep rancher with a wife and two children. He was not happy about the prospect of having to leave his flock to tend a sawmill, but being the devout follower of the faith that he was, he willingly obeyed Young's directive. Moving his sheep herd to a location near the sawmill where he could watch them, Croslin minded his stock while he supervised the operation of the mine.

One day a portion of Croslin's herd strayed into an adjacent canyon. Worried that they might fall prey to a mountain lion, the shepherd placed another man in charge of the sawmill while he went to retrieve his missing livestock.

Croslin found his sheep grazing on some grass just below a rock ledge that protruded slightly from the side of a canyon wall. The location was in sight of the sawmill, which Croslin could see in the distance. As he rode toward his herd, Croslin was distracted by bright sunlight reflecting from the shiny surface of the ledge. Curious, he climbed to the outcrop and examined it closely. To his amazement, he discovered it consisted of a thick layer of quartz laced with pure gold! Breaking several pieces of rock from the ledge, Croslin placed them in his pocket and climbed down. Gathering his sheep, he herded them from the area and returned them to the main flock. Next he stopped at the sawmill, told the workers he would be away for a couple of days, and immediately departed for Salt Lake City, about fifteen miles east.

Late the next day, when Croslin was admitted to Brigham Young's quarters, he excitedly related the story of finding the gold. Placing the few pieces of gold-laced quartz in front of the Mormon leader, he told him that he believed a great fortune awaited them in the canyon adjacent to the sawmill. Young examined the gold closely and then, with a heavy sigh, returned it to Croslin and admonished the young man for being distracted from his assignment by the promise of wealth. Young told the sheepherder that at this time the settlers should channel their energy into growing crops, raising livestock, and constructing a fine city. He explained to Croslin that the time might eventually come when it would be appropriate to mine the gold, but until then such activity would bring nothing but bad luck. Narrowing his eyes and growing into a quiet yet tense rage, the Mormon leader said he would inflict his wrath on anyone who dared to remove the gold. He concluded by ordering Croslin never to mention the discovery to anyone.

Croslin was confused by leader Young's dictates, but decided to adhere to them, at least for the time being. Over the next few years, however, Croslin, in defiance of Young's admonition, showed his samples of gold to several of his relatives and friends, and told them that when the time was right he would return to the golden ledge and extract enough of the ore to make himself wealthy. When Croslin's brother-in-law pressed him for information on the location of the gold, the shepherd said only that he could stand in the doorway of the sawmill and look into the canyon where the ledge was located.

Eventually, Rowberry returned as overseer of the saw-mill and Croslin went back to herding his sheep. Several weeks later, while he was moving his animals to a pasture in the canyon next to the mill, he visited the location of the golden ledge. Making certain he was not being observed, Croslin decided to remove some of the ore. His intention was to come to the canyon from time to time, remove a little of the gold with each visit, and store it until such time as Young removed the restrictions and he could exchange it for cash. All afternoon as his sheep grazed nearby, Croslin dug enough gold to fill a saddlebag.

Returning home that evening, Croslin informed his brother of what he had done and showed him the gold. When he offered some of the gold to his brother, the sibling backed away from it, stating that when the orders of

Brigham Young were violated a curse had been placed on the gold. Croslin laughed at his brother's response, returned the gold to the saddlebags, and hid it beneath a loose floorboard in his house.

The following morning as Croslin rode out to his sheep herd, his horse was spooked by a rattlesnake. Croslin was thrown to the ground and killed instantly as the result of a broken neck. Within days, Croslin's brother spread the story that the shepherd was killed because of the curse placed on the gold by Young. In 1861, Croslin's brother-in-law decided to search for the mysterious ledge of gold. He had heard Croslin speak of it on many occasions, and believed that with a little luck he might be able to find it.

Apparently he did. The brother-in-law was found dead a week after he left to find the ledge. His body was discovered at the mouth of the canyon adjacent to the saw-mill, and the pockets of his trousers were filled with several pounds of gold-laced quartz! Rumors of Brigham Young's curse once again began to spread throughout the area.

In 1864, another man undertook to look for the cursed ledge of gold. Bill Hickman, once a Mormon of high standing, had fallen into disfavor with Brigham Young and had been expelled from the valley. Before leaving, Hickman visited Croslin's widow in an attempt to learn the location of the ledge of gold. The widow could only relate what little information she had gleaned from her late husband, but Hickman believed it was enough to enable him to locate the rich ledge.

It is believed by many that Hickman found the gold, for he showed up in Lander, Wyoming, a few weeks later with a sackful of rich ore. Within two months, however, Hickman was found dead, and to this day the cause of his passing remains a mystery. Residents of the valley of the Great Salt Lake quietly spoke of the curse.

The tale of Croslin's cursed ledge of gold has been handed down over the many generations that have come and gone since it was discovered. In recent times, two of

Croslin's descendants learned of the story and, using an old map and journal they discovered, decided to search for what they believed would be a fortune in gold. One day the two appeared in Salt Lake City with several pieces of gold-laced quartz they claimed to have found in a canyon in Black Rock Ridge. After exchanging the gold for currency, the two young men got into a fight over the division of the money. One was killed, and the other fled from the area and has never been seen again.

Many who currently live in the area of the Great Salt Lake are familiar with the story of Croslin's cursed ledge of gold. A few claim to know exactly where it is located, but all are in fear of the dreaded curse and refuse to approach it. Although Brigham Young was buried more than a century ago, many of his faithful followers believe the eccentric leader can still reach out from the grave to punish those who defy his commands.

WYOMING

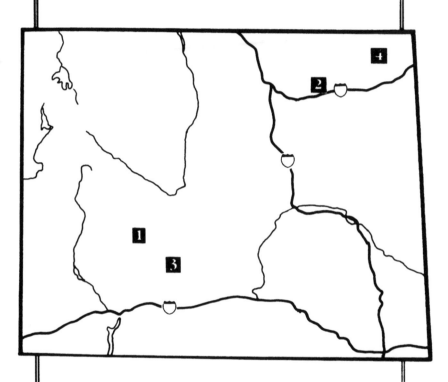

1. The Lost Cabin Gold Mine
2. Lost Bighorn Placer
3. Ella Watson's Buried Fortune
4. Lost Ledge of Gold

The Lost Cabin Gold Mine

The Wind River Range in western Wyoming boasts some of the most rugged country in the state. Snow-capped mountain peaks in excess of twelve thousand feet high are not uncommon, and they overlook dozens of deep, remote canyons, many of which remain relatively unexplored to this day.

In 1842, six years before the great strike at Sutter's Mill in California, gold was discovered in the Wind River Range, gold which lured several hardy and adventurous souls into this remote area which was home to hundreds of Indians. Some few found wealth, many more found only disappointment, and several found death. One of the gold discoveries in the Wind River Range may have been as rich as the greatest of the California strikes, but its location was lost more than a hundred years ago and has never been found. The gold, which apparently exists in impressive quantities, is still there.

The first gold discovered in the Wind River Range in 1842 was found by a trapper. Georgia Tom McKeever came west several years earlier to try to earn his fortune trapping beaver and selling the pelts to hat manufacturers in St. Louis, but McKeever found little but bad luck during his stay in the Rocky Mountains. Originally a member of a party of seventeen trappers, McKeever worked hard and added to the rapidly growing accumulation of pelts which the men believed would make them all rich. Three of the trappers, however, had other plans. While the rest of the group were setting traps in the ponds and streams in the Absaroka Range, the three loaded up the accumulated furs and made off with them.

Disheartened, the remaining trappers nevertheless continued their efforts for another three months until they eventually put together a second impressive collection of beaver pelts. Just as they were preparing to transport the skins to St. Louis, their camp was attacked by Indians, and all but Georgia Tom McKeever were killed. McKeever pretended to be dead, then crawled away from the camp in the dark of night and spent the next three weeks hiding in the mountains and trying to find his way back to civilization. Eventually he reached a settlement where he recovered from his ordeal.

Next season, McKeever decided to try trapping one more time. Alone, he rode into the Wind River Range to lay traps along the numerous streams. This range was normally avoided by most trappers because of the presence of hostile Indians, but that did not deter McKeever.

McKeever found the trapping in the Wind River Range disappointing. Though he diligently ran his lines and checked them every day, his take was pitifully small. One day, while searching for a new location in which to set traps, McKeever decided abandon trapping as a way of life and return to farming in Georgia. As he was exploring a new canyon, he saw a flash of color in the bottom of a narrow, shallow stream. Closer examination revealed the presence of gold nuggets in large quantities in the gravel bottom and, using only his hands, the trapper retrieved several of them.

For nearly three weeks, McKeever panned gold from the narrow stream until he ran out of containers in which to carry it. As winter was setting in, he decided to take what he had, leave the mountains, and return to Georgia.

Many days later, McKeever stopped at Fort Laramie in southeastern Wyoming and exchanged two large nuggets for cash. When asked where he got the gold, the trapper provided directions to the rich stream in the Wind River Range. Several of the hangers-on around the fort became excited about the prospect of finding gold in the western mountains, and the next morning saw nearly twenty men with pack animals loaded down with mining equipment setting out from the fort. Because of the Indian threat, however, the soldiers ordered them to return.

In 1863, two of the would-be prospectors from Fort Laramie were drinking beer in a tavern in Walla Walla, Washington, when they met a man named Allan Hurlburt. Hurlburt had arrived in California in 1849 to find gold, but had had no luck. He wandered northward over the years, prospecting and working at odd jobs along the way, until he arrived in southeastern Washington.

One evening, while taking a meal at the tavern, Hurlburt overheard the two prospectors relating the tale of Georgia Tom McKeever. Intrigued, Hurlburt introduced himself to the two men and pumped them for more information about the gold in the Wind River Range.

The next day, Hurlburt and two friends named Freitag and Smith left Walla Walla for the Wind River Range. They led six pack horses loaded with mining tools and provisions.

For weeks the three men roamed the mountains and canyons of the Wind River Range searching for some sign of gold. On several occasions they had to remain in hiding for days at a time due to the presence of Indians.

One evening in August of 1863, the three friends set up camp about fifty yards from a narrow, swiftly running stream, and quietly prepared dinner. They had learned to camp far from the noise of running water because the sound sometimes obscured other noises, such as those of approaching Indians.

Following the evening meal, Hurlburt carried the dishes to the stream to wash them. As he was finishing his chore, something in the stream bed caught his eye. Using a tin plate, Hurlburt scooped up a handful of gravel, washed it around in the plate, and extracted two large gold nuggets! Hurlburt called for his partners, and soon all three men were panning the gravel of the stream. They worked throughout the night under the light of torches, and by morning they had filled three pouches with nuggets of pure gold.

For the next several days, the men panned more ore than they ever dreamed they would find. Believing the gold came from a rich vein farther upstream, they determined to find it and retrieve even more gold than they were now taking in their placer operation.

About a month later, they discovered the vein. It proved to be very rich and the three decided that, with a few more months of digging the ore out of the rock matrix, they would be millionaires.

Because they had packed in an adequate supply of provisions, and because game was plentiful in the area, the three friends decided to remain in the canyon throughout the winter, working their placer operation and digging the gold from the rock. When the spring thaw arrived, they agreed, they would load their ore onto the pack horses and return to civilization.

To protect themselves against the harsh winters normally encountered in these high altitudes, the three men set to work constructing a log cabin on a flat spot not far from the stream.

The cabin was rude but adequate. Freitag constructed a large rock fireplace from the abundant flagstones found in the area. The hearth would provide heat and a place to cook. The roof of interlaced branches would protect them from all but the heaviest snowfalls.

Next to the fireplace they excavated a hole about two feet deep in which to store their gold. At the end of each day they would place the gold accumulated from the day's placer mining and excavation activities into the hole and cover it with a large stone. Hurlburt estimated the hole contained approximately a hundred thousand dollars' worth of gold nuggets.

One morning in the middle of October, Hurlburt remained in the cabin to chink the spaces between the logs with moss while Freitag and Smith left the cabin to work in the mine about a hundred yards upstream. The shaft had been excavated to a depth of six feet and the seam of gold grew thicker as they followed it. Around noon, Hurlburt heard rifle shots, but presumed one of the men had shot a deer.

When his partners failed to return to the cabin by sundown, Hurlburt grew concerned and went to look for them. On the way to the mine he called out their names but received no answer. When he reached the excavation, Hurlburt was horrified to find the mutilated body of his friend Smith—he had been scalped and all of his clothes save for his belt had been removed from his body.

Hurlburt looked around but could not find any sign of Freitag. Fearful the Indians might return at any moment, the terrified miner raced back to the cabin and gathered up his rifle and a few provisions. Just before leaving the cabin, he lifted the large stone from the hole, extracted two pouches of gold nuggets and put them in his shirt, replaced the stone, and fled.

For nearly a month Hurlburt wandered through the mountains, lost, cold, frightened, and hungry. He traveled at night and hid during the day. Because he couldn't see very well at night he had difficulty finding his way out of the mountains. He was afraid to shoot game for fear the Indians might hear him. Eventually he ran out of food and often went days without eating. Constantly traveling downhill in the hope of escaping the range, Hurlburt finally found himself walking along a road that led to Atlantic City, located near the southeastern tip of the range. A tinker driving a wagon found Hurlburt lying along the side of the road. Gaunt and delirious, his shoes worn to tatters, Hurlburt was suffering from frostbite on his fingers and toes. As the tinker placed Hurlburt in his wagon, he noticed that the semi-conscious man clutched tightly at two pouches of gold nuggets. By evening, the wagon had arrived in Atlantic City, where Hurlburt was treated for frostbite and malnutrition.

It took three weeks for Hurlburt to recover from his ordeal. When he did, he returned to Walla Walla where he lived with friends. Once spring arrived, however, he began to make plans to return to the Wind River Range, form a party of miners, and reenter the gold-rich canyon.

Because of the Indian menace in the mountains, no one would agree to accompany Hurlburt, so he foolishly entered the range alone. Remarkably, he found his way to the canyon and remained for three months living in the log cabin and panning gold from the stream. In September he rode into South Pass City with Smith's rifle and several pouches of gold nuggets stuffed in his saddlebags.

After showing the nuggets around town, Hurlburt once again attempted to organize a party of men to return with him to mine the gold, but as winter was setting in very few were interested. Discouraged, Hurlburt returned once more to Walla Walla.

The following spring found Hurlburt back at South Pass City. This time he successfully recruited four men and departed for the interior of the range. On this trip, however, Hurlburt was less fortunate. Time and again he became lost and could not find the canyon in which the rich, gold-filled stream and vein were located. Over and over he talked about the cabin, thinking he would find it in the next canyon, but eventually his four partners grew discouraged and the party returned to South Pass City after three months of fruitless searching. This time, Hurlburt announced he was giving up the search and returned to Walla Walla once and for all. Hurlburt's rich diggings were thereafter referred to as the Lost Cabin Mine.

In 1866, a man named Joe Poole wandered out of the Wind River Range with an intriguing tale. He had stopped in a tavern in South Pass City and heard several men talking about Hurlburt's Lost Cabin Mine in the Wind River Range. Poole became very interested and informed the men that he had just returned from a canyon that fit their description and had, in fact, found the skeleton of a man with a belt still tied around his mid-section near a narrow stream. Believing he had been close to the rich placer mine and ore vein discovered by Hurlburt, Poole bought a few provisions and returned to the mountains the next day. He was never seen again.

In 1886, a man named J.H. Osborne arrived at South Pass City after spending several months prospecting in the Wind River Range. He converted several large gold nuggets into cash, and when asked, told where he found them.

Osborne claimed he had been looking for color in the several streams he encountered in the range and finally found some in a shallow stream in a distant canyon. Spending several days in the vicinity, Osborne managed to accumulate several hundred dollars' worth of gold. He also found evidence of mining nearby, but neglected to examine the shaft closely. He told the listeners he stayed in an abandoned log cabin he found near the stream.

In spite of more than a hundred years of searching, no one has yet relocated the Lost Cabin Mine. The old log cabin has surely rotted and fallen down, but the sturdy rock fireplace has likely withstood the ravages of time. Several yards from the cabin runs a narrow stream replete with gold mixed in with the gravelly bottom, and farther upstream can be found the beginnings of an excavation which followed a rich, thick seam of gold into the rock. And adjacent to the old fireplace, in a shallow hole covered by a rock, lies a great fortune in gold nuggets, placed there more than a century ago by three men.

Lost Bighorn Placer

In the year 1865, a party of Swedish immigrants entered the Bighorn Mountains of north-central Wyoming in search of gold. Two years earlier the seven men had landed on the eastern shores of the continent, learned of the fortunes that hard-working and persevering men could make in the West, and decided to try their luck. They knew little about prospecting, but along the way they picked up knowledge and information as opportunities were presented and gradually learned a lot about ores and mining. When they entered the Bighorn Mountains, they brought with them two kinds of luck—good and bad. Good luck was with them when they discovered an incredibly rich placer mine in the mountain range; bad luck was inevitable, for the mountains were a refuge for the warring Sioux Indians and, unknown to the Swedes, had been declared off limits to all white men.

Riding across a sandbar in the middle of a slow-moving stream that bisected a broad meadow in the Bighorn Mountains, one of the Swedes noticed some sparkle coming from the ground. Dismounting, he inspected the sands and found them to be rich in flakes and nuggets of gold. Everywhere they looked on the sandbar, the Swedes found gold.

After nearly a year and a half of searching for the precious metal, the Swedes believed they had finally located the fortune they always hoped for. They quickly established a camp near the stream and spent every daylight hour panning for gold. Within the first week the men accumulated nearly twenty pounds of gold nuggets, flakes, and dust. At the end of each day they would divide the gold equally and place it in containers. As they sat around the campfire smoking their pipes, they spoke of the lives of luxury they intended to lead when they returned to Europe with their newfound riches.

The next day the snow began to fall and the Swedes decided it would be necessary to construct a cabin for protection against the freezing temperatures they knew would surely come. While two men continued to pan the gold, three commenced work on the cabin, while the remaining two went to hunt for game and lay in a supply of meat for the coming weeks.

Late that afternoon as the two hunters, each carrying a deer carcass, were returning to the cabin, they heard gunshots. Dropping the deer and crawling among the trees, the men approached the meadow and discovered their companions were under attack by Indians. As the defending Swedes fired from behind one wall of the unfinished cabin, the Indians rode back and forth in front of them, occasionally letting fly with an arrow. Knowing there was no way to go to the aid of their fellows, the two hunters remained hidden among the trees and watched.

Presently the Indians set fire to the cabin, forcing the Swedes to abandon its protection and run out into the open. One by one the miners were killed and their bodies mutilated. As several of the Indians scalped the dead miners, others ran into the burning cabin and retrieved some canned goods which they hacked open and ate.

For nearly three hours the two surviving Swedes watched the Indians from their hiding place, shivering from cold and terror. Eventually, the attackers rounded up the miners' horses and mules, mounted their own, and rode away to the west.

Cautiously, the two men crept toward the ruins of the smoldering cabin. Poking through the remains, they found their store of gold—several thousand dollars' worth packed in empty baking soda cans. Placing some of the gold in their packs, they quickly fled the site of the carnage toward the southeast, and several days later arrived at Fort Reno near the Powder River.

The Swedes related their plight to the post commander, who expressed little sympathy. He scolded them for ignoring the treaties which forbade white men to enter the Bighorn Mountains. The two Swedes, unaware of the existence of such treaties, pleaded with the officer to provide an escort for their return to the placer mine. When the officer refused, the Swedes attempted to organize a civilian party to reenter the mountains and mine the gold, but the army blocked their efforts and threatened to jail the two men if they persisted in their plans.

The Swedes remained at Fort Reno throughout the winter. When spring arrived they traveled to Rapid City, where they believed they would be able to recruit a group of men to return to the Bighorn Mountains. The Swedes explained to the men, about a dozen altogether, that though the mountains were off-limits to whites, the gold they would find in the sandbar located in the remote high meadow would make the risk worthwhile.

Two months later the party clandestinely entered the Bighorn Mountains and was never seen again. Unknown to the men, Sioux Indians in great numbers were at that time taking refuge in the Bighorn Mountains, and it is presumed that once they became aware of the presence of the miners, they killed them.

By the time the Indians were subdued and removed to reservations years later, most people had forgotten the tale of the rich, gold-laden sandbar in the Bighorn Mountains. Occasionally some old prospector would enter the range, hoping he would be the lucky one to stumble onto the site, but in the intervening decades the gold has never been found.

Ella Watson's Buried Fortune

For several years before she was hanged one summer afternoon in 1899, Ella Watson had buried approximately fifty thousand dollars in gold and silver near her residence in the Sweetwater River Valley in southwestern Wyoming. Watson's fortune, the proceeds from selling stolen cattle, has remained lost since that time.

Ella Watson was not the kind of woman normally found in frontier Wyoming. Experienced in robbery, rustling, and various hustles and cons, Watson was a large woman, a dead shot, and a match for any man. After running away from her family's Kansas farm when she was fifteen, Watson wandered throughout the West, eventually ending up in Wyoming. Moving from town to town, she developed a keen instinct for survival and quickly discovered how easy it was to separate a drunk man from his money. She eventually fell in with a gang of cattle thieves, and for several years pocketed an impressive amount of money from selling stolen livestock.

Watson's travels took her to the Sweetwater River country, where she met Jim Averill. Averill had arrived in Fremont County in 1885 looking for a job. Unable to find honest work, he started rustling cattle, driving them to another part of the state and selling them. During the next several months, he made enough money to build a saloon on a well-traveled road near the Sweetwater River. As his business prospered, Averill built a large corral behind the saloon in which to keep his stolen livestock. Small-time rustlers often stopped by Averill's establishment and, over a period of time, he got to know many of them and eventually hired several to steal cattle for him. The rustlers would take a few head of livestock at a time from local herds and when they had a sufficient number gathered, would drive them to Cheyenne to sell. All profits were returned to Averill, who would then pay off the rustlers.

Shortly after Watson met Averill, the two set up housekeeping in a cabin located about two miles from the saloon. Because more and more people traveled the Sweetwater River Road, and because the saloon became increasingly popular, Averill was afraid someone might recognize the stolen cattle he kept out back. He decided to construct a new corral, adjacent to the cabin, so the animals would be far from the curious eyes of his customers.

Averill was eventually appointed postmaster for this slowly growing area, and this additional job kept him busy to the point that he turned the entire cattle rustling operation over to Ella, and all transactions were conducted at the cabin. Ella would contract with the rustlers, receive the stolen cattle and place them in the corral, and when the time was ready she would hire some cowhands to drive them to the railhead at Cheyenne.

One afternoon, Ella looked up from her household chores and spotted a lone rider out near the corral. The stranger was slowly circling the large pen and staring intently at the livestock it contained. Presently he rode away and Ella went back to her work.

About an hour later, two men in a wagon followed by four more on horseback rode up to the front door of the cabin. As the dust settled around them, they called for Ella to come out onto the porch. When she did, they informed her that the cattle she had in her corral had been stolen from them and they had come to retrieve them.

After cursing the newcomers, Ella went back into the house and returned with a pistol. Just as she stepped out the door, two of the men grabbed her, wrestled her to the ground, and took her firearm away. Tying her securely, they threw her into the back of the wagon and rode to Averill's saloon.

With guns drawn, two of the cattlemen entered the building and returned with Averill. He, like Ella, was bound and then placed alongside her in the back of the wagon. Without locking the empty saloon, the entire party rode toward a cottonwood-lined bank of the Sweetwater River. Along the way, one of the men interrogated Ella about her cattle rustling activities and learned she had buried just over fifty thousand dollars' worth of gold and silver coins in a secret location near the cabin. The man said that if she turned the money over to them, she and Averill would be set free. Averill, listening in on the conversation, hissed at Ella to keep quiet and assured her the men were only bluffing and that no harm would come to them.

Several minutes later the wagon pulled up under a large, spreading cottonwood. As two of the men prepared nooses, Averill and Ella were pulled to a standing position in the back of the wagon. Ropes were thrown over a low-hanging limb and the nooses placed over the heads of the two prisoners. The leader of the cattlemen repeated the offer to spare their lives if they would reveal the location of the buried gold and silver. Ella was now very frightened and was about to tell him where to find the cache, when Averill once again insisted to her that nothing was going to happen and that the men were just trying to scare them.

After the nooses were secured around the necks of Averill and Watson, the men jumped from the wagon, leaving the two cattle thieves standing side by side at the ends of the ropes. When Ella and Averill declined for the third time to reveal the location of the buried cache, one of the cattlemen lashed at the wagon's team, causing it to bolt away. A few seconds later, Ella and Averill were swinging under the cottonwood limb, their lives being slowly choked from them by the constricting nooses. Within a few seconds they were both dead.

The cattlemen then returned to Ella's cabin and retrieved their livestock. While four of them drove the cattle toward the east, two remained to search the property for the cache, but could find nothing.

Over the years, others have traveled to the Averill-Watson cabin in search of the gold and silver, but all have reported failure.

About thirty years following the hanging of Averill and Watson, a letter from Ella to her family in Smith County, Kansas, was discovered in an old trunk. The letter, apparently written only a few weeks prior to her death, detailed her rustling activities and her love affair with Jim Averill. Obviously trying to impress the relatives she had fled years earlier, Ella, in a nearly illegible scrawl, told of the money she had earned by stealing cattle and how she had hidden a small fortune in an abandoned well near the cabin. Ella's letter, discovered in 1929, eventually came into the possession of a man who was familiar with the Sweetwater River country and the tales of local cattle rustling activities. He also knew the location of the old cabin in which Ella had lived.

When he arrived at the site of the Averill-Watson cabin, he was disappointed to discover it had been torn down and the surrounding land turned into pasture. Though he searched for hours, he could find no evidence of an old well. With the passage of time it had apparently been filled in and grown over with grass.

The gold and silver coins hidden a hundred years ago by Ella Watson still lie about six feet below the surface. Today the fifty thousand dollars in gold and silver coins that was buried during the 1890s would be worth considerably more. If someone were lucky enough to find the location of the old abandoned well, they would never have to work another day in their life.

Lost Ledge of Gold

Around 1870, Deadwood, South Dakota, was a bustling community catering to the miners who explored, prospected, and extracted gold ore from the nearby Black Hills. Deadwood was a collection of unpainted wood frame buildings and shabby tents in which prospectors and miners could find liquor, women, and gambling, as well as supplies. Many a prospector arrived in Deadwood bearing a sack of gold nuggets and announced a rich discovery someplace back in the remote and often dangerous hills. Many more wandered into the town discouraged and broke, having failed to find even a glimmer of gold.

One of the strangest tales of gold discovered and subsequently lost came from a grizzled old prospector named Boggs. The old man arrived in town one afternoon, disoriented and confused. He wandered up and down the main street as if trying to get his bearings, when he was recognized by another of his kind. Hailing the old man, his friend invited him into the nearest saloon for a drink.

At the bar, the companion asked Boggs how things were going out at his claim. The old man reached into his pockets and pulled out a handful of gold-filled quartz rocks and laid them on the bar. Several patrons quickly gathered around the old-timer to examine the gold; all were curious as to where it came from. When they asked him questions, the old man could only respond with a blank stare. Presently, he sat down at a table and related a most unusual story.

About a year earlier, Boggs had arrived at the Bear Lodge Mountains in northeastern Wyoming, just southwest of Devils' Tower, a prominent landmark. The old man panned the streams and inspected outcrops, ever searching for gold. One day, Boggs entered a narrow canyon he had never seen before and worked his way up toward the head of it. As the canyon narrowed and the incline increased, Boggs, tired from the climb, found a fallen log on which to rest. Suddenly he noticed a thin ledge of different-colored rock protruding from one wall of the canyon. On closer inspection, he happily discovered the ledge was an outcrop of gold-laced quartz. Boggs dug out several small pieces and found them to be the purest gold he had ever seen. The vein, according to the old man, extended for several feet in either direction. Truly, he thought, here was enough gold to make him as wealthy as a king.

For several months Boggs dug the gold from the quartz matrix, accumulating an impressive amount of the ore. When he was not working his mine, he busied himself with the construction of a small, crude rock cabin at the mouth of the canyon. Behind the cabin, Boggs dug a shallow trench in which he placed and covered up his gold.

Deadwood was located some twenty-five miles to the east, and it was during a trip to town to purchase some supplies that Boggs met a young lawyer named Burns. The old man and the lawyer became friends and Boggs would always stop to visit during subsequent journeys into town.

During one visit, Boggs asked Burns if he would like to accompany him into the mountains. At first the lawyer demurred, but Boggs was insistent and finally the young man gave in. The next morning, the two rode out of Deadwood and into the Bear Lodge Mountains, where Boggs told the lawyer about his gold discovery and took him to the ledge. Burns knew very little about mining, but he recognized gold when he saw it. Staring at the ledge, Burns saw plenty of the ore and suddenly realized Boggs was a very rich man.

After remaining with Boggs for nearly a week, the lawyer returned to town, his pockets filled with several pieces of gold-bearing quartz from the old prospector.

A few weeks later, Boggs decided to take a break from mining and go deer hunting. He had seen plenty of deer sign in a neighboring canyon, so he decided to ride over there. While riding along a particularly rocky stretch of ground, Boggs's horse slipped on some loose stone, panicked, and threw his rider. Boggs landed on his head and was knocked unconscious for several hours. When he finally awoke, it was dark. Looking around, Boggs had no idea where he was. Leaving his gun and hat on the ground, the old man rose and walked out of the canyon. Daylight found him wandering in the range, searching for some familiar landmark, but the blow he received on his head apparently had affected his memory. He was unable to find his way back to the cabin and the canyon that contained his rich ledge of gold and his buried fortune. Days later Boggs—tired, hungry, and filthy—somehow wandered into Deadwood, where he was recognized.

One of the men at the saloon knew that Boggs was a friend of Burns's and sent for the lawyer. When Burns arrived, he corroborated Boggs's story of the rich gold mine. Taking Boggs home with him, he placed the old man under the care of a physician and saw to his comfort.

As Boggs recovered during the next few weeks, he continually expressed a keen desire to return to the Bear Lodge Mountains and relocate his gold mine. When he was well enough to travel, Burns outfitted the old man with a good horse, a pack mule, and adequate supplies. Three weeks later, however, Boggs was back in Deadwood. He informed Burns that he could remember nothing about the mountains or the location of the canyon, that he had become lost and confused, and had finally given up.

Burns decided to accompany Boggs on a return trip to the mountains in search of the gold, but like the old prospector, he too became lost and confused. After a month of fruitless searching, the two abandoned the mountains and returned to Deadwood.

Over the next few years, several others made attempts to locate Boggs's mysterious canyon. At one time, there were nearly a dozen prospectors combing the Bear Lodge Mountains searching for a small rock cabin at the entrance to a narrow canyon.

One man did find the cabin, but at the time he was unfamiliar with the tale of Boggs's lost gold ledge and hurried caching of the ore. As he explained it in later years, the prospector had spent several weeks in the Bear Lodge Mountains panning some small streams. Quite by accident, he entered a narrow canyon he described as little more than a ravine. Just at the entrance of the canyon, he said, he discovered a low, crudely constructed rock cabin. So well did the structure blend into the surroundings that the prospector was within ten feet of it before he recognized it for what it was. Thinking someone might be about, he called out several times but received no answer. Assuming the canyon was the domain of whomever lived in the cabin, he rode away.

In the annals of Western history, the Black Hills of South Dakota were judged as one of the richest gold-bearing locations ever discovered on the North American continent. The Bear Lodge Mountains, located just across the border in Wyoming, are part of the same igneous core and share the same characteristics as the Black Hills. Though prospecting and mining in the Bear Lodge Mountains never compared to that which took place in the Black Hills, the gold ore that was occasionally discovered there proved to be quite pure and assayed at top dollar. Old man Boggs undoubtedly stumbled onto an incredibly rich lode in the Bear Lodge Mountains, but as a result of bad luck, lost it.

To this day Boggs's lost ledge of gold has not been found, nor has the cache of ore he buried behind his rock cabin.

Selected References

Anonymous. "The Lost Adams Diggings." *Colorado*, March-April, 1972.

Atwater, Jane. "Lost Wells-Fargo Gold." *Desert Magazine*, April, 1954.

Baier, Edward D. "The Lost Mine of the Bear Lodge Mountains." *Lost Treasure*, May, 1980.

Bailey, Tom. "Three Rocks, Two Graves, and a Fortune in Gold." *True West*, January-February, 1961.

Byerts, W.H. *Gold: The Adams Gold Diggings*. San Francisco: Frederic F. Hollister, 1988. (Reprint of pamphlet published in 1919 by W.H. Byerts, El Paso, Texas).

Carson, Kit. "That $100,000 Loot in the Malpais Country." *True West*, July-August, 1962.

Carson, Xanthus. *Treasure!* San Antonio: The Naylor Company, 1974.

Clark, Howard D. *Lost Mines of the Old West*. Los Angeles: Ghost Town Press, 1946.

Dobie, J. Frank. "Fever for Gold." *True West*, December, 1958.

Eberhart, Perry. *Treasure Tales of the Rockies*. Denver: Sage Books, 1961.

Forbes, William B. "The Lost Crazy Woman Mine." *True West*, May-June, 1961.

Hammer, C.G. "Lost Gold of the Lavas." *True West*, November-December, 1967.

Henderson, Randall. "Navajo Gods Guard the Silver of Pish-la-ki." *Desert Magazine*, December, 1950.

Hudson, Karl. "Lost Loma Gold." *Desert Magazine*, July, 1951.

Hult, Ruby El. *Treasure Hunting Northwest*. Portland: Binsford and Mort, Publishers, 1971.

_____. *Lost Mines and Treasures of the Pacific Northwest*. Portland: Binsford and Mort, Publishers, 1957.

Hunt, Charles B. *Natural Regions of the United States and Canada. San Francisco: W.H. Freeman and Company, 1967.*

Jameson, W.C. "The Curse of the Lost Sheepherder's Mine." *Lost Treasure*, May, 1992.

_____. *Buried Treasures of the American Southwest*. Little Rock: August House Publishers, 1989.

Kelly, Charles. "Lost Silver of Pish-la-ki." *Desert Magazine*, December, 1940.

Kildare, Maurice "Outlaw Loot in Missoula." *Frontier Times*, October-November, 1971.

_____. "Missing Gold Bars of Tres Piedras." *True West*, May-June, 1970.

_____. "Henry Plummer's Golden Loot." *Frontier Times*, April-May, 1965.

Latham, John H. *Famous Lost Mines of the Old West*. Conroe, Texas: True Treasure Publications, 1971

LeGaye, E.S. *Treasure Anthology, Volume I.* Houston, Texas: Western Heritage Press, 1973.

Lovelace, Leland. *Lost Mines and Hidden Treasure.* San Antonio, Texas: The Naylor Company, 1956.

Marshall, John B. and Cornelius, Temple H. *Golden Treasures of the San Juan.* Chicago: Sage Books/Swallow Press, 1961.

Mitchell, John. "Lost Apache Gold Mine." *Desert Magazine,* June, 1967.

Mitchell, John D. *Lost Mines and Buried Treasures Along the Old Frontier.* Glorieta, New Mexico: The Rio Grande Press, 1953.

_____. "The Pothole Placers." *Desert Magazine,* February, 1949.

Moore, Jean M. "Buried Treasure on the Little Big Horn." *True West,* July-August, 1960.

Murbarger, Nell. "Lost Hardin Silver: Mystery or Hoax?" *Desert Magazine,* April, 1955.

_____. "A Skeleton Guards the Lost Gold of Jarbridge." *Desert Magazine,* November, 1955.

_____. "The Lost Sheepherder Mine." *True West,* September-October, 1957.

_____. "Mystery of the Lost Hardin Silver." *True West,* September-October, 1961.

Paterson, J.H. *North America.* New York: Oxford University Press, 1989.

Penfield, Thomas. *Dig Here!* San Antonio: The Naylor Company, 1962.

Rascoe, Jesse Ed. *The Golden Crescent: The Southwest Treasure Belt.* Toyahvale, Texas: Frontier Book Company, 1962.

Rhea, W.D. "Pumpkin Seed Gold." *Lost Treasure,* Winter, 1967.

Rhoades, Gale. "Lost Rhoads Mine." *Frontier Times,* June-July, 1970.

Richardson, Gladwell. "Gold Behind a Waterfall." *Desert Magazine,* March, 1953.

_____. "Lost Mine of Coconino." *Desert Magazine,* July, 1950.

Rose, Milton. "Silver Mountain." *True West,* January-February, 1961.

Thompson, George A. *Faded Footprints: The Lost Rhoads Mines and Other Hidden Treasures of Utah's Killer Mountains.* Salt Lake City, Utah: Roaming the West Publications, Inc., 1991.

Townsend, Ben. "Hanged Woman's Treasure." *Lost Treasure,* April, 1976.

Weinman, Ken. "The Great Falls Train Robbery." *Lost Treasure,* May, 1991

_____. "The Lost Gold Bars of Tres Piedras." *Lost Treasure,* April, 1991.

_____. "Prison Window Treasure." *Lost Treasure,* December, 1988.

Williams, Brad and Pepper, Choral. *Lost Treasures of the West.* New York: Holt, Rinehart, and Winston, 1975.

Winslowe, John. "Lost River Mountains Mine." *True West,* January-February, 1972.